Dear Reader,

I had the particular pleasure of growing up with cousins—lots and lots of cousins. I can still remember spending summers hunting for frogs, running through barns, and playing hide and seek until it was too dark to see. There were no streetlamps where I grew up. We came inside when the mosquitoes got so thick that we could no longer fend them off. And the food? There were no greater feasts than the ones I enjoyed when all of the cousins got together and Dad and my uncles fired up the grill. Afterward, they always broke out the guitars, and my cousins and I would listen as our parents sang the songs from *their* childhood.

That's why I enjoyed writing about Jan and Elaine so much. The relationship between these two steadfast cousins reminded me of days gone by, when the only people who knew me as well as my sisters were my precious cousins. I learned life lessons alongside them, things like when to stand tough—and when to run. I learned to enjoy good food, to appreciate great music, and the importance of family.

All of these things are woven into the relationship between Jan and Elaine. Their love for one another is a tangible reminder of the gift I get to enjoy every day—the gift of family. I'll never take them for granted.

I hope you enjoy reading this book as much as I enjoyed writing it.

Blessings,
Elizabeth Ludwig

Tearoom Mysteries

TEAROOM
mysteries

The Tea
Will Tell

ELIZABETH LUDWIG

Guideposts
New York

Published by Guideposts Books & Inspirational Media
110 William Street
New York, New York 10038
Guideposts.org

Acknowledgments

Every attempt has been made to credit the sources of copyrighted material used
in this book. If any such acknowledgment has been inadvertently omitted or
miscredited, receipt of such information would be appreciated.

Scripture quotations are taken from *The Holy Bible, New International Version*.
Copyright © 1973, 1978, 1984, 2011 by Biblica, Inc. Used by permission of
Zondervan. All rights reserved worldwide. www.zondervan.com

Cover and interior design by Müllerhaus
Cover illustration by Ross Jones, represented by Deborah Wolfe, Ltd.
Typeset by Aptara, Inc.

Printed and bound in the United States of America
10 9 8 7 6 5 4 3 2 1

CHAPTER ONE

A breeze from one of the half-open kitchen windows stirred a corner of the newspaper Elaine Cook read, the rustling pages adding to the symphony of a quiet Saturday morning before the tearoom opened. Jan Blake was baking, so Elaine had wandered downstairs to sit with her.

"The lake looks calm today." Jan's voice cut through Elaine's musings.

"Yep," she said, without looking up.

Jan's rolling pin made a thumping sound against the marble counter. "It would be a perfect day for a walk along the shore. We should have time before we open."

"Probably."

"Would you like to come along?"

"Good idea."

"Elaine?"

"Huh?"

"I asked if you would like to come along."

Elaine looked up to find her cousin staring at her, a small smile curving her lips. Jan lifted her hand and made a walking motion with two fingers. "Around the lake. A walk. You and me. Want to go?"

"Oh." A blush warmed Elaine's cheeks. "I'm so sorry. I was just so wrapped up in this article."

Jan closed the oven door and walked over to look. "What article?"

Elaine turned the newspaper so Jan could read the headline.

"String of Home Invasions Strikes Lancaster." Jan sat in a chair next to Elaine's. "Home invasions...as in robberies? How dreadful."

Elaine lowered the paper and eyed her curiously. "You heard that one of the homes broken into was Priscilla's, from the library, right?"

"Priscilla's?" Jan's eyes widened. "No, I had not heard that. She and I haven't had a chance to talk since the last book club meeting. She went out of town to visit some relatives, I think."

Elaine nodded. "It happened right after she got back. Lucky for her, she was working late at the library trying to get caught up from her trip when it happened. I shudder to think of the outcome had she been home alone."

"Oh, Elaine, that's so terrible. No wonder you were caught up in that article. Does it say anything else about the other homes that were broken into?"

"Only that there have been five break-ins so far," she said, handing Jan the paper. "But it does have some interesting information. See for yourself." She pointed to a picture included with the article. "The only information police are releasing is that the robber is armed and considered dangerous. That's a replica of the gun there."

Jan frowned. "How do they know what gun was used?"

"Apparently, they were able to use some video tape captured by the security system in the home of one of the other victims. The article says police are not releasing the actual photos yet because the investigation is ongoing."

The front door opened. Elaine poked her head into the hall and saw Archie Bentham step in, his cheeks ruddy and his white hair standing on end. He slipped out of his beige jacket and hung it on the hall tree next to the door.

"Good morning!" their employee called, his voice chipper.

"Morning, Archie," Elaine said. She ducked back into the kitchen. "Archie's here." This time, it was Jan who barely lifted her head.

Archie ambled into the kitchen and made his way to the coffeepot. "Smashing weather we're having."

"I hadn't noticed. I was too caught up in this article." Elaine cast a glance through the window toward the lake, where white froth danced atop the waves. "Anyway, I'm glad the weather is nice. Jan and I were thinking of taking a quick walk before the tearoom opens."

"Well, take a jacket." Archie rubbed his hands together briskly. "It *is* only September, but there's already a slight nip in the air. I wonder if this weather means we're in for a long winter. If so, we'd better stock up on ice melt."

Elaine laid her finger against her lips. "*Hmm*…I wonder if the temperatures will mean we'll have a good crowd. Labor Day is on Monday and most people will have the day off."

"We should have a respectable turnout." Archie eyed the trays of baked goods lining the counter, then joined them at the table and pulled out a chair. "It's probably a good thing you and Jan had the foresight to prepare a few extra cookies and scones."

Elaine pointed to her cousin. "That was Jan's idea. She thought we should have them on hand, just in case."

Finished with the article, Jan blew out a breath and laid the paper down. She looked over her glasses at Archie. "Oh, hello, Archie. When did you get here?"

Archie threw a puzzled glance at Elaine.

"Never mind her," she said, giving a wave of her hand. "You've heard about the string of break-ins hitting Lancaster, haven't you, Archie?"

"I have, but I haven't paid them much mind." He tapped a corner of the newspaper. "Is that what has Jan so engrossed?"

"Uh-huh." Jan smoothed her hand over the paper, then reached for her cup. "I realize we are hardly immune to crime here in our little corner of Maine, but I surely never imagined it would happen to someone as sweet as Priscilla."

"Priscilla Gates's house was broken into," Elaine explained to Archie, "along with several others."

Archie scratched his head. "That's terrible. Was she hurt? Was anything taken?"

Elaine shrugged. "She wasn't home when it happened, and I really don't know if anything was taken. I'll have to ask her next time I see her."

"Oh." Jan's mouth puckered as she lowered her teacup. "My tea is cold."

"Please allow me." Archie rose and swept up the cup and saucer in one hand.

"Thank you, Archie," Jan said. "There are fresh cranberry scones on the counter if you'd like one. In fact, I wish you *would* sample one. I'm trying out a new recipe."

Archie dipped his head playfully in her direction. "Madam, it will be my honor."

The cousins chuckled at his antics and then Elaine waved toward the window. "What about our walk? Still want to go?"

Jan checked her watch. "It's only quarter after eight. I just put the last batch of cookies in the oven, but they should be done…"

The timer rang as if on cue, and Jan rose to transfer the cookies from the oven onto a cooling rack. "Never mind the tea, Archie. Elaine and I will be going outside as soon as I finish up here." She worked quietly a moment, then slid her hands from a pair of oven mitts and laid them on the counter. "There. That's all of them. I think we'll have time for our walk now if we make it brief."

Jan went to fetch a sweater for herself and one for Elaine. Elaine was thankful Archie had suggested it because the sun's pale rays did little to add warmth.

She jammed her arms into the sleeves of her cardigan before turning for the path that led down to the shore and a dock that stretched out into Chickadee Lake. Next to her, Jan did the same, only she also buttoned her sweater up to her neck.

"Archie is right. There is a nip in the air."

Elaine chuckled. "Maybe we'll get lucky and have one last Indian summer before the really cold weather hits."

"I hope so. This air isn't good for my skin. It gets so dry in the winter." Jan blew out a breath. "You know, Elaine, I didn't just want to go for a walk. There's something I've been meaning to talk to you about."

"Oh?" Elaine glanced at her sidelong. Jan's tone was troubled, and for her normally cheerful cousin, that was odd. "Is everything okay?"

Jan shrugged deeper into her sweater. "I'm not sure. This thing with Bob's new job in Baltimore has me in knots."

Elaine's heart sank. "So he's still bent on taking it? He hasn't reconsidered after you turned down his proposal?"

Jan's eyes widened behind her glasses. "He still says it's... it's the opportunity of a lifetime."

Her words drooped at the end, as though she'd tried desperately and failed to convince herself of them. Elaine slowed her steps. They had reached the edge of the lake. Tall rushes and trees grew here, and provided homes to a variety of fowl and wildlife. They took refuge alongside the lake, just as she and Jan had done when they bought the tearoom, but now...

She reached out to touch Jan's shoulder. "I'm sorry. I know this is difficult."

Jan sniffed and pulled a tissue from the pocket of her sweater. "It's just... I thought..." She shrugged. "Well, you know. I'd hoped Bob and I would get married. But I can't give up the tearoom, and he is set on leaving, so I will just have to make do."

Helplessness crept over Elaine like fog. She didn't like seeing Jan so forlorn, but what could she do?

"Look there." She pointed at one of the black-capped chickadees that their lake was named after. The pretty little thing was perched on one of the tall rushes and seemed content to study them, his small head tilting from side to side.

"Oh, he's beautiful." Jan pressed her hands together in delight. "No wonder the people of Maine chose those little fellows as the state bird."

Elaine smiled, struck by a sudden thought. "Well, he's not a sparrow, but I figure God's eye is on him too, wouldn't you think?"

Jan gave a slow nod.

Elaine draped her arm around her cousin's shoulder. "I think we can use the reminder."

Slowly, a bit of the tension relaxed from Jan's features. She turned to look at the bird, which chose that particular moment to soar off into the sky. "You're right, of course. And I suppose if that one tiny bird is important to Him…"

"You can rest assured that you are too." Elaine gave Jan's shoulder a squeeze, then dropped her arm. "God will find a way to work this all out. In the meantime you just have to have faith. You know I'll be praying for both you and Bob."

"I know, and I'm grateful," Jan said. Lifting her glasses, she wiped her eyes with the tissue and then pushed it back into her pocket. "Well, I suppose we should be getting back. Archie is going to wonder where we've gone."

Elaine smiled, relieved to see a bit of the spunk return to Jan's blue eyes. "So you do think business will stay steady, though most of the tourists have gone?"

She nodded. "How can it not? I've been baking all morning and I'm pretty sure I left the kitchen window open a crack. The scent should be all over Lancaster by now."

Though it was silly, Elaine took a deep whiff and nodded. "Yep, I smell it now. We'd better get back before the tearoom fills up and Archie storms off in a huff."

She offered her elbow to Jan, who took it and turned with her back toward the house.

"So you haven't told me recently, how are things with you and Nathan?" Jan eyed her slyly. "You realize that with Bob out of the picture, I'm going to take an inordinate interest in the two of you."

Elaine laughed and patted Jan's hand. "There's nothing much to tell, really." Her face warmed despite the cool morning air. "Okay, so the truth is things are progressing. I just never thought…that is, after I lost Ben, I never thought…"

She sighed, and Jan laughed. "Isn't that how it always works? When we aren't even thinking about it, and when we least expect it, that's when love happens."

Love?

Elaine bit her lip. She certainly cared deeply for Nathan, but could she call it love? She pushed the thought to the back of her mind as she and Jan reentered the tearoom.

Elaine took off her sweater and put out her hand. "Give me your sweater. I'll take it upstairs with mine."

Jan complied, and Elaine took her time heading up the stairs. She really was going to have to give this whole thing with Nathan some serious thought. After all, dating was one thing, but to say she was in love was quite another.

Thinking about love dredged up all sorts of old memories, including her first encounter with Ben—the excitement, the tingling in her veins, the lightheaded giddiness that left her walking on air. Her feelings for Nathan were different, of course—she'd been in her twenties when she and Ben met. Was the difference in her feelings for Nathan simply that she was so much older and more mature, or something else?

By the time she returned to the east parlor, it was almost time for the tearoom to open. Rose Young, their other employee, was busy putting sugar bowls on each of the tables. Elaine tied a frilly cabbage rose apron that she'd found at a garage sale around her waist, then hurried to do the same in the west parlor.

At ten o'clock sharp, Elaine went to unlock the door. Within minutes, the tearoom began to fill with regulars and new visitors alike. Business was so good, in fact, that the morning passed in a blur. Thankfully, Rose and Archie were light on their feet. Rose's smile remained fixed in place as she took care of customers in the east parlor, while Archie handled the west. Elaine managed the cash register, and Jan poked her head out of the kitchen from time to time to help clear tables.

It wasn't until almost two that any of them had a chance to catch their breath. What happened to the lull that normally occurred around lunchtime? Not today. None of them had dared take a break and Elaine's stomach rumbled in protest. She drew her arm across her brow wearily. Across the tearoom, Archie lifted his hand and motioned to her. As she approached, he pointed to the hall and the kitchen that lay beyond.

"You should sit down, Elaine. You haven't stopped or even slowed down once since we opened."

"Well, being behind the cash register helps," she said. "You and Rose did far more running than I did."

His scowl remained fixed in place as he propped his hands on his hips. "The crowd has thinned some. Have you eaten?"

Elaine hesitated and cast a long glance toward the kitchen. "Not yet, but I was just about to let Jan know that Jo Murphy called requesting two dozen ginger chews. The twins are having friends over tonight, and she doesn't have time to bake. I need to ask Jan if she has that many available before I call Jo back."

"I can take care of that. You take this into the kitchen and sit awhile." Archie held an empty teacup and saucer toward her and looked at her insistently until she took them.

"Fine, but I'll make it quick so you can eat too." Elaine turned gratefully for the kitchen. "My aching feet will never be the same after this day."

Archie chuckled. "Well then, I suppose it's good fortune for both of us that we've only a couple of hours left before we close."

"Indeed."

He patted his stomach. "Jan said she's got sandwiches made for everyone. I'm thinking about taking her up on her offer. I'm sure they'll be delicious."

Elaine's mouth watered thinking about the loaf of homemade bread she'd seen Jan taking out of the oven early that morning, but she hated making Archie wait.

She shook her head. "Tell you what, why don't you go on? I'll stay out here and wait on these last few customers. The minute they finish, I'll come in and join you."

"Elaine…"

"Archie, I insist. I couldn't enjoy my lunch otherwise." She pressed the cup back into his hands.

His eyebrows lifted as he hesitated. "What about Rose? Perhaps she could watch the front."

"I told her I would let her go early." Elaine hid a wry smile. "She has a big test coming up that she has to study for and I felt sorry for her."

Rose was in culinary school, and though she loved her classes, Elaine knew she was worried about her test.

Archie headed off toward the kitchen, and Elaine passed the time chatting with the customers who were left in the tearoom. One couple was from Texas, and had come to Maine to visit family. Another woman had traveled all the way from California and stumbled on the tearoom by accident. Elaine enjoyed listening to people explain how they'd come to arrive in Lancaster, and was filled with a satisfied sort of tired when at last she locked the tearoom door.

As though she'd been cued by the click, Jan emerged from the kitchen. Her hair stuck out oddly in various places, and flour dusted her glasses and her nose. In her hands, she bore a plate piled high with chips and a turkey sandwich that made Elaine's mouth water. "Well now, that was…"

"A rousing success?" Elaine laughed and joined Jan and Archie at one of the tables. "Please tell me that sandwich is for me."

Jan laughed and placed it in her hands. "You've earned it. We've already eaten ours."

"Thank goodness." Elaine started to sit, then eyed the few remaining tables that had yet to be cleared in the east parlor. She looked at her sandwich longingly and then back at the stacks of dirty dishes and teacups. "I suppose I should…"

"Don't even think about it," Jan interrupted. "Archie and I can clean up while you eat."

It was all the prompting Elaine needed. She dropped into the chair and took a healthy bite.

"There were a fair number of regulars here this morning," Jan said, moving to the nearest table and gathering up the tea-cups. "Didn't you think so, Archie? I know I saw Kit and Russell Edmonds here, and I think I spied Patti Garland. She ordered a maple croissant, didn't she?"

He nodded. "Though I thought the number of tourists was impressive too."

They continued chatting as they moved from one table to the next while Elaine munched happily on her sandwich. She picked up a chip. "And did you notice that Macy Atherton didn't have one critique this morning? She must have really liked your cranberry scones today."

She laughed and then popped the chip in her mouth, savoring the crisp snap and savory saltiness—a perfect comple-ment to her scrumptious sandwich.

"I'll have to keep that in mind." Jan laughed and carried a tray of dishes toward the kitchen.

There was some clattering from the kitchen, and then Jan returned empty-handed. She paused in the hall near the cash register. "Say, what's this?"

She bent and picked up a brown paper bag. "It's heavy. Did someone leave it in the tearoom?"

Elaine squinted. There were no markings to distinguish the bag from any other. She shrugged. "I have no idea. Archie, did you see who left that bag?"

Across the room, Archie shook his head. "No, sorry."

"*Hmm.* I suppose I should look."

Jan pulled open the bag to peer inside. Something about the look on her face arrested Elaine's chewing mid-bite.

She swallowed hastily. "Jan? What is it?"

Jan looked up slowly, her eyes wide with disbelief. "It's..." Her gaze returned to the bag.

"What?" Not liking the pallor that had come over her cousin, Elaine persisted. "What did you find?"

Archie looked up too. "Jan?"

Jan's finger shook as she pointed. "It's a gun, Elaine. Someone has left a gun in the tearoom."

CHAPTER TWO

S haking took hold of Jan's limbs as she set the bag containing the gun quickly onto the floor. "What do you mean it's a gun?" Elaine's face registered shock, disbelief, morbid curiosity...all of the same things Jan felt.

Elaine stood, upsetting her teacup. A small beige stain spread on the tablecloth. It would require a good soak if she didn't want the stain to set, Jan thought—as if there wasn't anything else going on.

"Jan, step away from that bag," Archie said. He stretched out his hand, his fingers twitching as he motioned her to a safe distance.

His sharp tone was enough to jerk Jan from her paralysis. She moved into the comforting circle of Elaine's arms.

"Are you sure it's a gun?" Elaine whispered. Her eyes narrowed and she peered at the bag as though the weapon inside might go off at any moment.

"Well, I wasn't married to a military man like you were," Jan joked, her sense of humor returning, "but I'm pretty sure I could recognize a gun."

Instantly, Jan felt Elaine's arms relax.

"You're right, of course." Elaine stepped forward and poked at the bag with a puzzled frown. "How do you suppose it got here? Did you see who left it?"

"I didn't. You probably would have had a better chance of witnessing that when whoever left it checked out."

"I suppose," Elaine said, "except it was so busy in here, I wasn't paying attention. We must have had a hundred people come through." She turned to Archie. "What about you, Archie? Did you see anything?"

He shook his head. "We could ask Rose, I suppose, see if she remembers seeing that bag."

All three stared at the bag in silence.

"It's not going to move on its own, I guess." Jan bent and picked up the bag by the edges and carried it gingerly to the east parlor and the nearest table. Setting it down carefully, she pushed open the sides so that they could all look inside.

Archie's head bobbed. "That's a gun all right."

"Do you know what kind?" Elaine asked.

The bag rustled as he pushed it open wider. "No idea, though I confess, my areas of expertise don't extend toward weaponry—unless you count medieval swords." He lifted one finger. "And some Far East swords. I did a study once on the shoguns of Japan. They carried some fantastic..."

"Archie!" Elaine and Jan exclaimed in unison.

"Right. Sorry." He lowered his head humbly. "No, I don't know what kind of gun it is."

Jan blew out a slow breath. "What do you suppose we should do with it?"

"We'll have to contact the police, of course." Archie snapped his fingers.

"Yes, we should. I'm sure Dan Benson will know what to do."

Elaine nodded. "I agree, but first, I sure would like to get a better look at it."

She reached for the edge of the bag. Jan quickly snagged her grasping fingers.

"Elaine, do you think we should?"

Elaine's teeth worked her bottom lip. "Well, what if it has a name engraved on the handle or something? Or maybe there's a paper in there with it. We could find out who it belongs to just by taking a closer look."

Jan considered that a moment then reluctantly removed her hand and watched while Elaine lifted the bag and gently shook the gun out. It made a clunking sound as it settled onto the table. Jan adjusted her glasses higher on her nose and bent in close. The gun was silver with a black handle, but apart from a few markings on the barrel, there was nothing to indicate who it belonged to.

She pulled back. "Do either of you see anything?"

Archie and Elaine both shook their heads.

"No name that I can see," Archie said.

"Maybe we should flip it over," Elaine suggested.

Jan grabbed her arm before she could reach for it. "Wait. Use this." She handed her one of the tearoom's linen napkins. "Just in case…you don't want to leave fingerprints."

Jan and Elaine exchanged a glance. Though neither of them had voiced it, there was mutual concern that the weapon they'd found in the tearoom could have been left by a criminal.

Elaine flicked the napkin open with a snap of her wrist. "Good thinking, Jan. Thank you."

She turned the gun over carefully.

Jan pointed to some numbers engraved on the barrel. "What is that? *75. AUTO. CAL.* What does that mean?"

"I'm not sure what the number seventy-five signifies," Archie said. "'Auto' stands for automatic, and the 'cal' stands for caliber."

"Nine millimeter?" Elaine pointed to more etchings on the barrel.

"I think so," Archie said. "And look there...it says it's manufactured in Italy by Kimar."

"So it's an Italian gun?" Jan asked.

He scratched his temple. "It must be, though I suppose we'd have to check with a gun expert to be certain."

A shudder traveled down Jan's spine. "I just can't believe anyone would wander off and leave something like this behind. Why do you think...?"

A soft click cut off the rest of what she'd been about to say. Next to her, Elaine lowered her phone to take another picture.

"Good idea," Jan said.

"Maybe we can send it to a gun expert...Oh!" She broke off and grabbed Jan's arm. "I just remembered something."

Jan laid her free hand over her heart. "Goodness. What did you remember?"

She turned her head side to side frantically. "The newspaper from this morning—do you know where it went?"

Archie walked over to the cash register and reached into the shelf underneath. "Here it is. I put it away for reading later."

Elaine snatched the newspaper. It rustled loudly as she jerked it open.

"What on earth are you looking for?" Jan asked.

Elaine's head dipped as she scanned the cover page. "Ah ha! Here it is." She smoothed the paper onto the table and pointed. "Look at that picture. What do you see?"

Jan's mouth dropped open. Archie's did the same.

"You see it too. It's the same gun." Elaine's gaze bounced from Jan to Archie. Her voice dropped to a whisper. "Whoever is behind these home break-ins was here in our tearoom."

CHAPTER THREE

For several seconds, no one spoke.

Slowly, Elaine stepped away from the paper, shock swirling through her belly. "We need to get Dan over here right away in case whoever left this"—she motioned toward the gun—"decides to come back for it. Then again, they might not want to risk blowing their cover. They have to realize that once their gun is found, it wouldn't take long to tie it to the robberies."

Jan's eyes widened behind her glasses. "But that...that can't be right. The same criminal who's been breaking into people's houses came into our tearoom for tea and cookies?"

Archie pointed toward the paper. "We have the proof right here."

Elaine held her phone aloft. "Let me pull up Dan's number." She scrolled quickly through her contacts. "Here it is."

Jan and Archie stared at her, both wearing matching looks of amazement.

She lowered the phone slowly. "What are you two staring at?"

Archie blinked. "Do you realize that one of us spoke to the thief? One of us knows who they were with and what they look like."

"That could be dangerous," Jan added.

Archie nodded. "Especially if word gets out we found that gun."

Jan's hand fluttered to her throat nervously. "We should be careful."

Suddenly, Elaine felt a little sick. She grabbed her phone. "You're right, both of you. Let's call Dan and get that thing out of the house."

"And one of us should call Rose to see if she remembers anything," Jan said.

Elaine agreed, and they quickly placed the calls. Once she told Dan why she'd called, he disconnected with a promise to be there as soon as possible.

Elaine laid her phone gently on the table. "Okay, he's on his way."

"And I spoke to Rose. She doesn't remember seeing anything unusual, but she said she'd be happy to speak to Dan if she needs to. Did he say how long he'd be?" Jan paced to the front door, checked the lock, and paced back. "What should we do in the meantime?"

"He didn't say how long he'd be, but I'm sure he'll hurry."

The clock above the fireplace chimed the half hour. Had it only been thirty minutes since they closed?

Elaine shook her head. "We should do something to keep busy while we're waiting." She turned her gaze to Archie. "Do you think you could find someone who can tell us about the gun?"

He rubbed his chin thoughtfully. "I think so. I met a man a few years back, on one of my excursions through Italy. He was an antiques dealer and owned a shop there, but he also collected old and restored guns. He's very knowledgeable. I'm sure he could tell us something."

Elaine plucked her phone from her pocket, typed in Archie's phone number, attached the photo of the gun, and hit Send.

"Wonderful. I just sent you a copy of the picture I took of the gun. Can you contact him?"

He scratched his temple. "Of course, though it may be some time before he gets back to us. The man was like a bloodhound when it came to sniffing out treasures and could often be gone weeks at a time. That's how he and I met, in fact. We were both at an estate sale for an old *conte* who'd passed away and left his family penniless."

"Well, we can at least try," Elaine said. "Make sure to include the phone number to the tearoom when you e-mail him, just in case he needs to call. Do you know his address?"

Archie shook his head. "I'm afraid not. I'll have to go home and dig it out of my old files."

Elaine checked her watch. "Dan should be here soon, but you may have time to get it before he arrives. Why don't you go ahead and go so you can start looking?"

His eyebrows bunched and he rubbed his temple doubtfully. "Are you sure? I would be glad to wait with you."

Elaine shook her head firmly. "I'd rather not waste any time. Besides, I'm sure we'll be fine until he arrives, right, Jan?"

"Of course." Jan crossed to the cash register and took a notepad out from under the counter. "And while we're waiting,

Elaine and I will create a list of everyone who came into the tearoom to give to Dan."

Archie didn't look quite so certain, but he fetched his jacket from the hall tree and poked his arms into the sleeves. "All right then, I'll head back here as soon as I've found it. You'll call me if you hear anything else?"

"Of course," Elaine said.

She sent him off with a wave and then joined Jan at one of the tables, glad she had thought to put together a list for Trooper Benson. He would most certainly ask, and they could get a considerable head start working on it while they waited for him to arrive.

Jan scribbled furiously for a minute and then looked up at Elaine. "I've written down several of the regulars I saw come in. Do you think you could fetch the receipts from today so we can write down any names we don't know?"

"That's a good idea," Elaine said, rising to get them, "but you realize several people paid with cash."

"Yes, but I think it will help to give Dan as many names as we can."

"You're right."

Elaine laid the stack of cash register receipts on the table next to Jan's elbow. When she finished writing, Elaine pulled the first one off the top and read the name.

"Diane Blanchett."

"I remember. She ordered the oatmeal raisin cookie with a cup of oolong."

Elaine added Diane's name to her list with a little dash and a note that said "Regular."

"There's no way Diane is our criminal," Jan explained, "but I think Dan is going to want to know everyone who was here so he can question them about the gun. Who knows? One of them may have seen who left the bag."

Elaine tossed a teasing glance at her cousin. "Very clever. You're so good at this." She read several more names, some that were already included on the list, and a few that Jan had to add.

"That's it," Elaine said, laying the last receipt atop the stack. "Now, can you think of anyone who came in that we haven't already mentioned?"

Jan bit the top of her pen. "*Hmm*...did I see Frank Conrad come in?"

"The music teacher?" Elaine nodded quickly. "Yes. Rose waited on him, but you're right, he was here." She touched the paper with her index finger. "There was also a couple from Texas. Oh...what was their name?" She tapped her fingers to her temple, thinking. "Robinson, I think. Or Robertson. Something like that. They're here visiting family."

"Shouldn't be too hard to track down." She jotted their name along with a note about their family. When she finished, she stared at the paper a second and then put her finger to her lips. "You know, there was this man I spoke to who seemed a bit odd."

Elaine's ears pricked. "Odd, how?"

Jan immediately backtracked. "Maybe *odd* isn't the right word. He just seemed a little preoccupied." She made a pecking motion with her finger. "He was always checking his phone."

Elaine chuckled and relaxed against the back of her chair. "That's not so odd nowadays."

"No, but when I tried to make small talk, he acted like he was suddenly in a hurry to leave. And, Elaine, he said he's not from around here, yet he knew an awful lot about Lancaster."

Intrigued, Elaine leaned forward. "What do you mean?"

"Well, he asked if I knew of any hotels in Waterville because all of the cottages along the lake were full—probably because of Labor Day. Anyway, I asked if he'd checked the Northwoods Bed-and-Breakfast. It struck me that he seemed a bit surprised that there was a business in town that he hadn't heard of, but when I started to give him directions, he just kind of waved and said he knew his way around."

"*Hmm.* That is a little strange. Did he give you a name?"

Jan didn't hesitate. "Henry Philpott. I remember because of his last name." She made a pouring motion. "Fill pot?"

"Oh, I get it." Elaine nodded and pointed to the paper. "Okay, write him down."

Jan did and then looked up at Elaine. "What about you? Anybody strike you as strange?"

Elaine sighed and rubbed her eyes. "There were just so many people in the tearoom today."

"I know, but try to remember if there was anyone who maybe stood out to you."

She thought a minute, then nodded slowly. "There *was* this one couple—a young man named Matthew and a beautiful young woman with a strong Russian accent. I believe her name was Irina. I remember thinking she seemed upset about something."

"Upset, how?"

"They were arguing, maybe? I was trying not to eavesdrop, but I couldn't help seeing her wipe tears from her eyes as she left. The man left right behind her in quite a hurry." She reached for Jan's arm. "Do you think maybe that's what happened? I mean, he could have set the bag down when he came up to the register to pay but forgot all about it in his hurry to catch up with Irina."

"It's very possible," Jan said, the excitement in her voice matching Elaine's. She wrote "Matthew and Irina" on her paper and underlined the names. "Now, who else?"

Elaine snapped her fingers. "Oh, before I forget, write down foreign tourist with bodyguard."

"What!" Jan fumbled with her pencil and nearly dropped it. "Foreign tourist with a *bodyguard*? Are you sure?"

"I think so." Elaine fought a sudden surge of uncertainty. "I mean, that's what it looked like. The man—bodyguard—was large and severe looking." She motioned to her eyes. "And he was wearing a pair of those dark shades like the aviators and police officers wear. He all but spoke into his watch."

Jan appeared fascinated as she listened. "What about the other guy, the foreign tourist? What did he look like? Was he wealthy?"

"He *acted* wealthy." Elaine snorted and sat back in her chair. "He barely looked at me and when he did, it was sort of snooty and impatient. I actually expected him to order the most expensive thing on the menu, but instead he ordered a cup of black tea with lemon. He drank it straight too. No sugar."

Jan's mouth puckered in disgust. "Well, there's no accounting for taste, I suppose."

"I guess."

"You said he was foreign. Any idea where he was from?"

Elaine touched her ear. "The accent was familiar, what I heard of it from the conversation he was having with his bodyguard. He sounded like he was from one of those Eastern European countries."

"Really?" Jan tapped her pencil against her lips, thinking. "Very strange that we should have two Eastern European visitors in the same day, don't you think?"

"I know…"

She broke off as a long shadow darkened the window seat. It couldn't be Archie. He wouldn't have had time to get home and return, but no one else had knocked. Startled, she turned wide eyes toward Jan.

"Jan," she whispered, clutching the edge of the table to keep from shaking. "There's someone on our porch."

CHAPTER FOUR

J an pressed her hand to her chest in a feeble attempt to
calm its erratic beating. The long shadow wavered and
became even more menacing as it drew closer to the window. "It could be Dan," she murmured. She took a breath
and began again, stronger. "It must be. He said he would be
over straightaway."

Elaine turned wide eyes toward her. "Then why didn't he
ring the bell?"

Since she didn't have an answer, Jan simply reached for
Elaine's hand and held on tight. "Maybe we should call someone," Jan said, her voice a quivering whisper.

"Who? Dan is already on his..."

Suddenly, a face appeared in the window. Elaine shrieked
and clapped both hands over her mouth. Jan simply froze, too
paralyzed for a moment to realize that the blue eyes and tuft
of sandy blond hair poking out from under a Boston Red Sox
baseball cap did indeed belong to Dan Benson.

He smiled and waved through the glass before bending low
to scoop something up. When he straightened, he held Earl

Grey, the finicky feline looking quite smug and comfortable in Dan's arms.

Elaine dropped her hands to her sides. "Oh good heavens, it's just Dan with the cat!"

Jan released the air from her lungs in a whoosh. She moved to the front door and undid the lock. Dan met her there. With two fingers, he tickled Earl Grey under the chin.

"Look who I found. A runaway."

Jan nodded. "Would you mind carrying him around to the back? I'll open the screened porch."

"Sure." Dan smiled and carried Earl away, the conniving cat winking at Jan over his elbow until they disappeared from sight.

Jan closed the front door and locked it up tight before moving down the hall, through the kitchen, to the back door. She felt better now that the trooper was here, but she'd be gladder still to be rid of the gun resting on their tearoom table.

The screen door squealed as she pushed it open to allow Dan in. Jan pointed toward a cushion in the corner. "Go ahead and set him down. Over there is fine, thank you."

He obligingly deposited the cat onto the bed and then followed Jan into the kitchen. "Sorry it took me so long. I was actually on my way to Augusta when Elaine phoned."

"Were you on a call?" Jan asked, worried.

He shook his head. "Actually, I took the day off. I was headed that way on an errand."

Indeed, it wasn't just the baseball cap that wasn't part of his typical uniform, Jan noted. Dan stood on their screened porch in a pair of blue jeans and a black T-shirt. She paused at the kitchen door and put her hand to her mouth.

"Oh dear, I hope we're not keeping you from something."

He gave a wave of his hand. "This is far more important, and it'll keep me from having to cut my grass since I was heading to Augusta to buy a new lawnmower. Ours gave out last week. Lucky thing we're nearing the end of summer." He chuckled. "Now, where is this gun Elaine said you found?"

Jan felt herself relaxing in the trooper's comforting presence. She breathed a silent prayer of thanksgiving for their local law enforcement as she led him into the parlor where Elaine waited.

"Dan, thank goodness you're here," Elaine exclaimed, apparently as relieved as Jan to see him. She motioned toward the table where the gun rested. "It's right over here."

"You didn't touch the gun, did you?" Dan cautioned.

Elaine gave another shake of her head. "Oh no. We don't want to risk disturbing any fingerprints or leaving new ones, so I just shook it out of the bag onto the table." She raised her hand. "But only because we thought we should take a closer look at it in case we could figure out who it belonged to. Was that all right?"

Though she had her own fingerprinting kit and was familiar with its use, Elaine wrung her hands nervously while she waited for the trooper's reply.

"That's fine, Elaine." He eyed the gun a second and then the bag that it had come from. A strange expression crossed his face, almost contemplative as he bent near for a closer look. "This is the gun you found this morning?"

Elaine's head bobbed rapidly. "And then we saw this." She grabbed the newspaper and laid it on the table next to the gun. "It looks like the same gun as the one used in the break-ins."

"It certainly appears similar," the trooper agreed. He motioned toward the bag. "And you said it was in this sack? Can you tell me where you found it?"

Elaine motioned toward the register and quickly recounted the events that had led to Jan's discovery.

Jan suddenly experienced a moment of panic. "Oh dear, I just realized I *did* touch the bag when I carried it over to the table."

Dan shook his head. "Don't worry, we couldn't have lifted any fingerprints off of that crumpled bag. It would have to be a smooth, nonporous surface for us to get any kind of distinguishable mark." He cupped his chin. "I am quite intrigued by this gun, however. I'm glad you called me."

He pulled a handkerchief from his pocket and used it to deposit the gun back into the paper sack. When he finished, he pushed the handkerchief back into his pocket and straightened. "Now, what can you tell me...?"

Jan handed him the list she and Elaine had compiled.

"...about the people who passed through the tearoom this morning." Dan smiled. "I should have known you two would know what to do."

"Thank you," Jan said. "The regular customers are on one side, and people we don't know are on the other." She touched the paper with the tip of her finger. "I also added a little star next to the people Elaine and I thought were acting a little odd."

He glanced over the list and then folded it in half. "Nice work, ladies."

Elaine nearly glowed under his praise. "Are you going to need us to come in for questioning?"

"Not necessarily. I'll call you if I have any questions for you." He picked up the bag and moved toward the door.

"Thank you for coming, Dan." Jan relaxed her shoulders, relieved now that the gun would be gone and she and Elaine could go back to business as usual in the tearoom.

"It was my pleasure. Of course, if anything suspicious happens, be sure to call me. Now have a good afternoon, and"— he tapped the lock on the front door—"you might want to keep this fastened in case whoever left this gun comes looking for it. I'll be sure to drive by a couple of times to check on you too."

"Absolutely. Thanks again," Jan said. She followed him to the door and slid the lock into place behind him, then turned to Elaine. "Well, that was certainly exciting."

Elaine frowned. "I suppose."

She smoothed her hand over a tablecloth, then picked up a half-empty cream pitcher and flitted over to the next table. "*Hmm.* I'd better get a tray to pick all of these up."

"Elaine."

"Yes?"

She eyed Jan innocently. Jan crossed her arms.

"You're up to something."

"Not at all. I was just thinking."

"About what?"

Elaine added a second pitcher of cream to the tray. "Oh, it's nothing really." She grabbed a towel and began wiping up a pile of spilled sugar. "It's just that I think I know where that man, the one with the bodyguard, is staying."

"How can you possibly know that? Did he say something?"

"Not exactly." Elaine's eyes sparkled as she set down the tray and rejoined Jan at the table. "I was working the cash register when his bodyguard came up to pay. When he took out his wallet, a card dropped out of his pocket. I only caught a quick glimpse, but it was enough to see it was blue and silver."

"Like the ones Karl uses over at Lake Country Cottages?"

Elaine nodded quickly. "They must be staying there. Why else would he have Karl's card?"

"A lot of the tourists stay over there." Jan frowned uncertainly. "It's one of the more popular rentals."

"I don't know about popular, but it's certainly one of the more expensive places."

"True, but what does that have to do with us?"

Elaine sighed and went back to cleaning. "Nothing, I suppose."

Jan watched as she wiped the same spot on the table a second time. "So," she said after a moment, "why are you still thinking about it?"

Elaine looked up and then at the towel. Chuckling, she picked up the tray and moved to another table. "Honestly, it's nothing more than curiosity."

"Curiosity?"

Elaine nodded. "Who was that man? What is he doing in Lancaster? He must be someone important if he needs a bodyguard." She planted her hands firmly on her hips and eyed Jan squarely. "Aren't you the least bit curious?"

"A little," Jan admitted, and then hurried to finish before Elaine could interrupt. "But not enough to go poking about. After all, what if he's the culprit behind the break-ins? Who knows what kind of danger we could inadvertently stumble into?"

Elaine's shoulders drooped. "You're right. I should forget about the whole thing."

"Good," Jan said, glad that her cousin was seeing sense. She reached behind her back and gave her apron strings a tug. "Now, if you don't mind, I think I'll run by the grocery store and pick up a few things I'm getting low on. Do you need anything?"

Elaine thought a minute and then shook her head. "No, I don't think so."

"All right, then I'll just…" She broke off at the ringing of her cell phone. "Oops, I think that's mine. Where did I leave it?"

Elaine pointed toward the kitchen. "Sounds like it's coming from back there."

"You're right." Jan hurried out of the parlor and down the hall. Her phone lay on the counter, ringing and vibrating toward the edge. She caught it a second before it went over onto the floor and swiped the screen to answer. "Hello?"

"Jan? It's Bob."

Jan's heart lurched. She had yet to reconcile herself to the fact that he would be leaving soon. At least when she was working, she could pretend that problem didn't exist. She forced a note of cheer into her voice. "Hi, Bob."

"Listen, Jan, I know I said I would come by later, but I'm afraid I'm going to have to change those plans."

Disappointed, she let her shoulders droop. "I'm sorry to hear that. I hope nothing's wrong."

His answer surprised her. "Unfortunately, Jan, there is. I'm afraid something is very wrong indeed."

CHAPTER FIVE

Though she tried not to, Elaine couldn't help but hear the note of disappointment in Jan's voice as she said good-bye to Bob and hung up. She waited a moment, and then carried the tray of creamers into the kitchen.

"Who was that?" she asked, though she'd very clearly heard Jan say it was Bob.

Jan set her phone onto the counter with a click. When she turned, her eyes were wide, her lips tight. "Forget about the store, Elaine. I'm going over to Bob's house and I don't know what time I'll be back."

"But I thought he was coming here." Elaine set the tray down and began pouring the unused creamer down the sink. "Is everything okay?"

Jan shook her head so hard she had to adjust her glasses. "Unfortunately, no. Bob just finished filing a police report. His house was broken into."

"What!" Elaine set one of the little pitchers of cream down so hard she cracked it. She crossed to Jan and took her by the arms. "When? Is he okay? Was he home when it happened?"

"He assured me that he is okay. In fact, he said he didn't even realize anything was wrong until this afternoon. The door leading to the garage was open a smidge, and when he went to investigate he noticed the jamb was splintered as though it had been forced open."

Elaine laid her hand against her chest. "I can't believe he didn't hear anything."

"Bob says it could have happened anytime, maybe even while he was gone to Baltimore, getting his new office ready."

Which would explain why he was only discovering it now. Elaine nodded. "So did he say if there was anything missing?"

Jan tapped her chin. "Not that he could tell. He still needed to report it though, seeing as how his house appears to be a part of the same string of break-ins that struck Priscilla." She shook her head. "Poor Priscilla. Bob sounded pretty upset over the phone. I can only imagine how frightened she must feel."

Elaine stiffened her spine. "You know, Jan, while you are out checking on Bob, I think I *will* drive by Lake Country Cottages, just to see what I can find out about that foreign tourist. Don't worry," she said, before Jan could convince her to change her mind, "I'll be careful." She brushed off her hands and turned from the sink. "I've been meaning to pay old Karl a visit anyway, just to see if he's at all interested in having us cater his grand unveiling of that renovation project he's been working on all summer."

"The dock and gazebo out over the lake?" Jan smacked her forehead in disgust. "I forgot all about that. I meant to call him last week."

"Don't worry about it," Elaine said reassuringly. "Besides, it's the perfect excuse to take a run out that way." She shook her finger at Jan. "You be sure and let me know what Bob has to say, all right? I'll check back with you this evening."

Jan bit her lip nervously. "I don't know, Elaine. Maybe you shouldn't go out there alone."

"Ah, but I won't be alone," Elaine joked. "I'll be with my old pal Karl. It'll be perfectly safe." She propped her fist on her hip. "Didn't you say you were going to check on Bob?"

After a moment, Jan nodded and then scurried to gather up her purse. "You're right. I'm wasting time. I'll be back soon," she said as she shrugged into her coat.

Elaine gave her word and shooed Jan out the door. Now that she had a reason for visiting the cottages, a twinge of excitement bubbled up inside her chest. She hurried upstairs for a light jacket and her purse before winding her way out to her car.

Cars were still parked in front of Sylvia's Closet, the vintage clothing shop next to the tearoom. Kate's Diner was also full, Elaine noted as she drove past. Apparently, all of the businesses in Lancaster were making out well this holiday weekend.

Elaine turned on to Cottage Road and headed toward Penzance, mindful of her speed as she passed the many cottage rental places tucked into the trees along the road. This time of year, bicyclists and skateboarders were liable to appear from either direction, and children camping with their parents often scurried out from the woods.

Spying the smoke from campfires rising, Elaine rolled down her window and took a deep whiff. Campfires always reminded her of her childhood—of roasted marshmallows and fireflies in a jar. Ben had understood that. He'd taught their kids to enjoy the outdoors from a young age.

Thinking of Ben brought a smile to her lips but a tear to her heart. She put up the window and pulled into the parking lot outside of Karl's Lake Country Cottages. Like the card she'd seen slip to the floor, the sign above the front door was a vibrant blue with the word "Office" painted in silver. Elaine pushed it open and stepped inside.

Like many of the businesses around Lancaster and Penzance, Karl's place capitalized on the lake theme. The counter and window frames were painted a crisp white. Offsetting the stark color were navy and gold accents in the furniture coverings and drapes. Above the office door hung an old wooden oar emblazoned with the word "Welcome," but it was the polished bronze ship bell next to the counter that fascinated Elaine the most. Above it was a sign that said "Please ring for service." She obliged and pulled the string.

Karl poked his head out of the office. "Be right with—oh. Hello, Elaine."

"Hi, Karl."

"Be with you in a moment."

"Take your time."

She gave a cheerful wave. He disappeared back into his office, and she meandered about the lobby. A large rack filled with flyers occupied one wall, and Elaine was glad to see the flyer she'd created for the tearoom among them. The number was dwindling, however, and she made a mental note to print more.

The trilling of her phone interrupted her thoughts. She pulled it from her purse and checked the ID. Archie? She picked up.

"Hello, Archie."

"Hello, Elaine. Just wanted to call and let you know I found that card for the antiques dealer I told you about. I'm sending him a brief e-mail now."

"Oh, that's wonderful, Archie. Thank you for letting me know."

"Did you hear from Trooper Benson? Do I need to hurry back?"

Elaine replaced the flyers and moved toward the window. "Indeed we did. He came by shortly after you left and collected the gun. Also, Jan and I made a list of everyone we could remember who was in the tearoom this morning and gave it to him. It'll take him some time to go over it, so don't worry about hurrying back. I'm sure he'll call if he needs to speak with you." She paused. "Say, Archie, you don't happen to recall a man with a foreign-sounding accent, do you? I believe he had a bodyguard with him."

"You mean the Czech? Yes, I remember him. He didn't talk much."

"The check?"

"From the Czech Republic."

A few yards away, the door to one of the cottages opened. Elaine watched with casual interest as a man stepped out. "Of course."

But now, Elaine diverted her attention from Archie to the person she saw crossing the driveway to a dark-blue Honda. He was wearing a hat and coat, but the figure reminded her of the bodyguard she'd seen in the tearoom. She leaned closer to the window for a better look.

"Uh…listen, Archie, I'm going to have to go. I'm at Karl's place now, and I think I see the man who was with the Czech earlier this morning."

"Karl's place?"

"Lake Country Cottages. You know—on Cottage Road? The man dropped a card when he came up to pay and I guessed maybe this was where they were staying. Looks like I guessed right." Elaine moved to the door. "I'll call you later, okay?"

"Elaine, wait. Why are you…?"

She didn't wait to hear the rest but disconnected when she saw the man tug a set of keys from his pocket. He was leaving?

She hurried outside, but instead of reaching for the car door, the man circled around to the trunk and pulled something out. Elaine slowed her steps.

"Good afternoon," she called out. She raised one arm above her head and waved. "Hello?"

The man paused, one hand braced on the lid of the trunk, the other clutching something at his side. With his arm raised, his jacket swung loose around his torso—what she could see through the gap in the trunk and the body of the car. The man wore a plain white T-shirt under his jacket, and a strange sort of holster the likes of which Elaine had only seen in movies. The leather strap attached to it fit snugly across his barrel chest. On impulse, she lifted her phone and snapped a quick picture, then jerked her hand to her side when the man slammed the trunk closed.

"Can I help you?" the man asked, his accent matching that of his friend from the tearoom. The man was blond and had a chiseled jaw that might have made her think him handsome had he not been glaring at her.

Elaine pasted a bright smile to her lips. "My name is Elaine. You and your friend came into the tearoom I run with my cousin this morning. Tea for Two?"

The man was much taller than Elaine. He looked even more intimidating as he squinted down at her from his lofty height. "Yes?"

Calling on the social skills she'd honed while living abroad with her husband, Elaine instantly began making small talk. "Beautiful day, isn't it? I'm so thankful the weather has improved. I bet you and your friend are really enjoying these cottages."

He didn't speak or crack a smile, so Elaine forged on.

"This is going to sound odd, I know, but I wonder if I might speak to your friend? He seemed so knowledgeable about teas, which of course is something I adore. I'm always trying to learn as much as I can about foreign and exotic teas. I thought I might sit down with him a bit, just to chat."

The man did not hesitate. "I am sorry, miss. He is unavailable at the moment. If you would excuse me?"

He gave a slight tilt of his head and then skirted around Elaine and made a beeline toward the cottages. In his hand was a black satchel, expensive by the look of the fine leather and polished silver buckles.

Elaine hurried after him. "Excuse me, sir? If you wouldn't mind, would you please give your friend my phone number? Perhaps we could meet at a more convenient time."

The man reached the cottage steps and whirled, halting Elaine in her tracks. Before he could speak, the door behind him swung open and the man she remembered from the tearoom stepped out.

"Pasha?"

Pasha—was that the bodyguard's name? The ogre turned and growled something in Czech. The man mumbled something back, then stepped around his friend and extended his hand.

"Please, you must forgive my friend. Pasha is, shall we say, zealous in his duties."

"No problem. I understand completely." She shook his hand and then touched her index finger to her lips. "Say, um, I was telling your friend we met earlier today. Do you remember?"

He smiled convivially. "Of course. Your tearoom was very quaint."

"Thank you." Elaine shifted her weight to her other foot and lifted her chin. "We haven't been formally introduced. My name is Elaine Cook."

"Bedrich Jagr." He let go of her hand. "It is a pleasure to meet you, Elaine."

"And you as well, Mr. Jagr."

He rocked back on his heels. "And now, we have done with the pleasantries, yes? What can I do for you?"

Elaine motioned toward the cottage. "Actually, Mr. Jagr, I was hoping you might have a moment to chat. I noticed when you were in the tearoom earlier today that you were very knowledgeable about teas."

He lifted an eyebrow and appeared to study her for a moment. Finally, he gave a small nod. "Yes, that is true. In fact,

I was about to have a cup. Would you care to join me?" He made a sweeping gesture with his arm.

Elaine nodded eagerly. "That would be wonderful. Thank you."

Mr. Jagr extended his elbow and Elaine slipped her hand through as they walked up the steps to the cottage.

"So tell me about your tearoom. How did you come to be the proprietor of such a wonderful place?"

"Oh, it's a long story," Elaine said with a chuckle. "But it started when my husband, Ben, passed away, just about two years ago now."

"I am sorry to hear this."

He motioned to a table near one of the windows. It was long and narrow, but charming in this cozy space. At one end of the room, a stone fireplace stretched toward the beamed ceiling. A large rug protected the beautiful oak floors, and comfy chairs invited one to sit and enjoy the view of the lake.

Mr. Jagr pulled out a chair and seated Elaine before seating himself opposite her. "Pasha, if you would not mind bringing the tea?"

The man gave a slight bow and disappeared into what Elaine assumed was the kitchen. She directed her gaze back to Mr. Jagr. "So . . . Pasha? Is that a European name?"

"It is Czech," he clarified proudly. "We are both from Prague. Pasha and I have been friends for many years."

"But he works for you?"

"He does. Unfortunately, my line of business requires that I surround myself with people I can trust. Pasha is one of the few."

"And what line of business is that?" Elaine asked. She didn't have to feign interest. She found herself more and more intrigued by Bedrich Jagr.

He rested his clasped hands on the table and appeared to mull his response carefully before he spoke. "I am a diplomat for my country."

"Really?" Elaine cast a glance out the window toward the rental car. "I didn't notice any diplomatic plates."

His expression darkened.

"My husband and I traveled extensively when he was alive," she said hastily, by way of explanation.

He shook his head and lifted one hand. "No, you are correct. I am not traveling in an official capacity, or the plates would of course be diplomatic. I am here on vacation."

"How lovely. How did you hear about Lancaster, of all places?" Elaine pressed.

Pasha returned bearing a tray laden with cups, a small china teapot, and a dish of sliced lemons. He set it on the table between them and then retraced his steps toward the kitchen, but not before bestowing on Elaine a wary glare.

Mr. Jagr motioned toward the teapot. "May I?"

"Of course."

Once again, he was drinking a simple black tea, Elaine noted. She recognized the strong scent instantly. Mr. Jagr's movements were elegant and precise as he poured a cup for her but he paused before passing it to her. "Forgive me. I did not think to warn Pasha. Perhaps you would care for some sugar or cream for your tea?"

Elaine waved her hand dismissively. "Lemon is fine."

He smiled appreciatively, his teeth perfect and white against his pale-olive skin. "Ah, that is good."

He set down her cup and extended the plate of lemons. Elaine plucked a wedge off the plate and gave it a delicate squeeze into her tea.

"So you were saying?" She laid the lemon wedge on the edge of her saucer. "About your visit to Lancaster?" she continued when he looked confused.

"Oh yes. I have a friend from here. He recommended this area and your lake as being very peaceful."

"Anyone I know?" Elaine asked. She took a sip of her tea and replaced the cup on the saucer.

"Oh, not here." He pointed toward the ground. "I mean Maine. My friend is from Bangor. We met many years ago. He was studying abroad."

"I see. It's nice that you keep in touch."

"Yes." He lifted his own cup and took a drink, then eyed her over the rim of his cup. "How do you like your tea?"

Suddenly, Elaine was reminded of every Hitchcock movie she'd ever watched. Her gaze dropped to her cup. Her heart rate was elevated, but that could just be because the man sitting across from her was a stranger, one with a very large and menacing friend. And she was sweating, but that could simply be due to the temperature inside the cottage. Was he running the heater?

"Mrs. Cook?"

Elaine looked up.

"Are you all right?"

"It's a little strong." Elaine motioned toward her cup. "The tea, I mean. It's a little strong."

He smiled seemed forced. "That is how we like it in my country."

His country...yes. Elaine leaned forward. "I would be so interested to hear more about your country. You said you are a diplomat. That must be so fascinating."

The smile seemed frozen in place. "Let us not discuss business, eh? You wanted to learn more about tea?"

"Yes, but that's before I heard about your job!" Elaine acted innocently, and as ditzy as she could. She pushed aside her cup to rest her arms against the table.

Mr. Jagr twisted his wrist to glance at his watch. "I am so sorry, Mrs. Cook. I have an appointment that I forgot all about."

He gave a flick of his hand. Elaine startled at Pasha's almost instant appearance. Had the man been listening just inside the kitchen door?

"Perhaps we can continue this discussion another time." He rose, one hand at his waist, the other stretched toward her.

Elaine rose with him.

"I certainly hope we can," she said, walking with him to the door. "And if I didn't say it before, thank you so much for your time"—she motioned toward the table—"and the tea. It was lovely."

He inclined his head slightly. "It was my pleasure."

He opened the door and then both he and Pasha followed her out onto the porch. She bade them both farewell and turned for her car. It took her a moment to locate her keys inside the deep recesses of her purse, and she couldn't help but notice while she searched the almost heated conversation that appeared to be taking place behind her. Though she couldn't understand the words, the tone was clear. Elaine risked a peek.

Pasha was indeed gesturing quite animatedly, and Mr. Jagr's face wore a deep flush. What interested Elaine even more was the glimpse she caught of Pasha. It was indeed a holster she had spied earlier, complete with a gun, the butt of which poked out from the edge of his jacket.

Elaine shivered as she pulled her keys from her purse and hit the unlock button. Mr. Jagr was a diplomat, so it made sense that the man accompanying him would have a gun, and yet...

Were her eyes playing tricks on her, or did the gun at his side resemble the one she and Jan had found in the tearoom?

Slipping her hand back inside her purse, Elaine withdrew her phone and snapped another quick picture. This time, Pasha noticed. His head jerked up and he glared across the short distance from the porch to the driveway where Elaine stood. His lips clamped shut, and his hands balled into fists. A moment later, he strode down the steps and came barreling straight for Elaine.

CHAPTER SIX

Elaine stood with her feet frozen to the driveway, her heart pounding inside her chest, as Pasha closed the distance between them. Like a thundering locomotive, he shuddered to a halt before her, his gaze skipping from her face to the phone clutched in her hand.

"What are you doing? What is that?"

"It's just my phone." Elaine shoved it into her purse, her hands shaking so that she almost missed and dropped it on the ground.

His eyes narrowed and he leaned toward her, his broad shoulders nearly blocking her entire line of sight so she saw only him. "You were taking pictures of Mr. Jagr. Why?"

"I was just...I...I merely..." Elaine retreated a step, her backside coming in contact with the door and hindering her from going further.

His scowl deepened. "Give me your phone. Now."

He jabbed his hand out, palm up. Elaine clutched her purse tightly to her chest.

"Is there a problem here?"

Nathan! Elaine spun her head around so fast, she nearly gave herself whiplash. Nathan climbed from his car and slammed the door shut, then made straight for Elaine. The air trapped in her lungs whooshed out, and she sagged against her car. Though Pasha did not look pleased, he did back off as Nathan neared.

"Nathan, thank goodness you're here," she whispered to him, and then turned to Pasha. "I'm sorry if I offended you. It's just that, in this country, people like to take pictures."

His head swung side to side stubbornly. "You must not take pictures of Mr. Jagr. Please, your phone."

Though he added the word *please* there was no entreaty in the hand he stuck out, fingers extended demandingly.

"Is this a matter of Mr. Jagr's security?" Elaine asked, emboldened now that Nathan stood beside her. And where was Mr. Jagr? She scanned the porch, but he was nowhere in sight.

Pasha hesitated and then his features softened. "Mr. Jagr is in Lancaster visiting for pleasure. If word got out of his presence, that would be gone. You see? He is a powerful man and powerful men often have enemies. I hope you will not jeopardize his stay or"—he squinted at her, his lips curved with disdain—"his life, for whatever small bit of attention you might garner on the..." He thought for a second and then snapped his fingers. "Facebook."

"Of course not." Elaine scrutinized his face but was unable, despite her efforts, to discern his sincerity. "I will not post the photos on social media."

Pasha nodded hesitantly, and grudgingly, or so it seemed. His lips pressed together firmly as he glanced at Nathan and then again at Elaine. "Very well. I will accept your word on this. Thank you."

He inclined his head slightly to them both before he whirled and strode back up the steps.

Next to her, Elaine heard Nathan blow out a sigh of relief. "Who was that?"

Now that he was gone, a tremor claimed Elaine's limbs. "His name is Pasha."

Nathan turned wide eyes to her. "Who?"

Elaine took his arm nervously. "I'll explain back at the tearoom. For now, let's get out of here."

"Elaine?" Karl called.

He motioned to her from the main building. Elaine waved back.

"Gotta go, Karl. I'll catch up with you later," she called.

Poor Karl, she thought as she climbed into her car. She hadn't even bothered explaining why she'd come. She'd have to remember to call him later.

Her tires spun on the gravel drive as she turned and drove out. Nathan followed closely behind. Bless him for appearing when he did. Elaine clutched the steering wheel tightly. That Pasha guy had seemed really angry. Who knew what might have happened had Nathan not shown up?

A few minutes later, she pulled into the garage behind the tearoom, but barely had time to open her door before Nathan was there. He pulled her into his arms, and Elaine was almost certain she could hear his heart hammering inside his chest.

"Are you all right?" he asked, his words muffled as he pressed his lips to her hair.

Warmth crept over Elaine, from her toes all the way up to her head. "I'm fine," she said, though really, her knees had only now stopped shaking. "Thank you so much for coming when you did."

"You scared me to death, you know." He drew back to grip her by the shoulders.

Elaine frowned. "Wait. How did you know that's what I was doing?"

He sighed and let his hands drop. "Archie told me."

"Archie? When did you talk to him?"

"About thirty minutes ago. I called to talk to him about his father's painting. He was really worried about you, you know. He thought maybe you were putting yourself in unnecessary danger. Judging by what I saw when I drove up, he was right."

"We don't know that for certain," Elaine countered, feeling bolder now that the situation was behind them. "Pasha was simply concerned for his boss, and I can't say as I blame him, considering Mr. Jagr's line of work."

"Who?"

"The man I actually went to see. His name is Bedrich Jagr. He's a diplomat from the Czech Republic."

"What's he doing in Lancaster?"

"Apparently, he's on vacation."

Nathan frowned. "On vacation? Here? How on earth did he hear about us?"

Elaine opened her mouth and then snapped it closed. "He said that he has a friend who lives in Bangor who recommended it."

"I was worried about you, Elaine." His face reddened as he spoke. Though he didn't say it, there was no doubting the concern she read in his eyes. She reached out and laid her hand gently against his rough cheek.

"I'm okay." Her heart fluttered as she held his gaze a moment. Finally, he gave a satisfied nod and motioned toward the house. "Well, I'm here. I might as well stay a while. Do you have plans for dinner?"

"I do now," Elaine replied teasingly. "Oh, but Jan probably won't be back in time. Did you hear about Bob?"

"What about him?" Nathan turned and led Elaine toward the garage entrance to the tearoom with a hand to her back.

"His house was broken into."

"What?"

Elaine nodded as she stepped into the hall by the office. Nathan followed her all the way through to the kitchen while she explained. "Jan is certain it's connected to the string of break-ins that have hit Lancaster, but since Bob can't pinpoint exactly when it happened, there's really no telling. It could be totally unrelated."

"Was anything taken?"

"I have no idea. I haven't spoken to Jan since she went over to Bob's." She crossed to the pantry and removed a jar of tomato sauce. "Spaghetti okay?"

"Sounds great." Nathan walked over to the sink and washed his hands. "So how many houses have been broken into?"

Elaine frowned and took out a box of pasta. "Five at the time the newspaper article was written, plus Bob's." She laid it on the counter next to the sauce. "I suppose I could call

Candace over at the *Penzance Courier*. She might be able to tell me more details."

Nathan agreed with a nod, then joined Elaine at the stove. "What can I do?"

Elaine pointed to a pasta pot. "Fill that with water? Oh, and I think there's a bag of salad in the refrigerator if you'd like to get it out and give it a toss."

Nathan did as she'd requested and then moved over to the counter to begin preparing the salad. Now that he appeared to have calmed some, Elaine felt comfortable asking exactly what Archie had told him.

"He pretty much filled me in," Nathan replied, wagging his finger at her. "The gun, the newspaper article, everything."

Elaine, slicing up a cucumber for the salad, paused to look at him. "What were you and Archie talking about anyway?"

Caught popping a cherry tomato into his mouth, Nathan widened his eyes and grunted, "Huh?"

"Earlier you said you called him to talk about his father's painting. What about it?"

Nathan chewed thoughtfully a moment. "Actually it was to tell him about an idea I had, or rather, an idea that was presented to me."

He grabbed a dish towel to dry his hands and crossed over to the stove where Elaine was adding a bit of salt to the pot of water for the pasta. "A lady came into the auction house with an old picture that had hung in her grandmother's house for years. She claimed it was by Jackson Pollock."

Elaine set the salt shaker aside and stared. "The famous American painter?"

"The same."

She couldn't help but gape. "That painting must have been worth thousands of dollars."

"Some of them can range that high," Nathan agreed. "Others have been known to value into the millions. This wasn't one of those," he clarified quickly. "It was a signed ink-on-paper portrait."

"But they're sure it was a Jackson Pollock?"

Nathan nodded. "The woman had already done all the legwork verifying the artwork. She provided me with a certificate of authenticity. Of course, the art market is flooded with forgeries, so this step was important. I would have no way of determining the portrait's value otherwise."

"This wasn't something you could authenticate yourself?" Elaine asked. Nathan had owned his auction house for several years, and he had a keen sense for the value of the items he put on display.

He shook his head. "When it comes to art, knowing the difference between a fake and an original takes years of professional experience, something I don't have." He shrugged. "In fact, I only know of a few reputable organizations who offer that level of expertise. This woman had a certificate from one of them. A friend of mine works there, so I checked that the certificate was valid." He paused and scratched his head above his ear. "Some of the major auction houses probably receive requests for authentication or appraisals every day, but unless they have professionals on staff who can offer a variety of authentication techniques, they risk some very serious liability."

The water for the pasta had begun to boil. Nathan grabbed the box of spaghetti and poured half of it into the pot. While he did that, Elaine grabbed a wooden spoon and laid it across the top of the pot.

"What's that for?"

"It keeps the water from boiling over," Elaine explained.

Nathan eyed the spoon in disbelief. "Really?"

Elaine waved her hand in amusement. "Anyway, about the portrait?"

"Right." He tore his gaze from the spoon. "I called my friend at the company who authenticated the woman's portrait. Along with materials dating, they check out the ownership history of a piece."

"Is that important?"

"It is, in fact, especially if you can trace a bill of sale back to the artist. Finally, they do something called Morellian analysis."

"What is that?"

Nathan laughed and crossed his arms. "I had to look it up myself. It's a process of distinguishing individual artists by the tiny idiosyncrasies or repeated stylistic details in their works."

"That makes sense. So what does all of this have to do with Archie?"

"Well, I thought if Archie could get the mystery painting authenticated..."

"He might finally be able to find out for sure if it is his father's work," Elaine finished thoughtfully. She twisted the lid off the jar of spaghetti sauce and poured it into a second pot to heat.

"Exactly." Nathan handed her a spoon to scoop out the rest of the sauce.

"So you gave him the contact information for the authentication experts?"

"I did, but…"

Arrested by the concern in his voice, she looked up.

"Unfortunately, Elaine, the place is in New York. Archie would have to take the painting there to have it authenticated."

She shrugged. "That's not a problem. I don't mind, and I'm sure Jan won't either. Who did you recommend?"

Nathan told her, and Elaine couldn't help but smile. It was the same company Heather Wells had recommended some time back when she and Jan first bought the painting. Apparently, they were all on the same page, and all just as curious to discover the mystery behind the painting.

JAN SPENT ALL of Sunday afternoon puttering around the kitchen, and thinking, and puttering some more. Her recipe box, which under normal circumstances could be counted on to provide a reliable diversion, proved completely useless. She stared at the words until they blurred. Her Bible study was only slightly more effective since she could barely concentrate and ended up reading the same passage over and over. Finally, exhausted by her circling thoughts, she decided to give it all over to God. When she finished praying, tears rolled down her face, but she felt better and a measure of peace had returned to her heart.

She swiped her finger under her wet eyes. At some point during her prayers, Elaine had quietly entered the kitchen and stood ready with a tissue. She pushed it into Jan's hand and then slid back a chair to join her at the table.

"Are you all right?"

Jan pressed the tissue to her nose. "I am now."

Elaine nodded. "I could tell something was bothering you at church this morning. You were so quiet. Why didn't you say something?"

"I wasn't ready, I suppose," Jan said, wiping the remaining tears from her eyes and rising to fetch a cup of tea for herself and Elaine.

"What about now? Do you want to talk about it?"

Concern creased Elaine's face and Jan immediately felt contrite. It wasn't fair of her to let her cousin fret so. She put a kettle on to boil and then went back to the table to sit next to Elaine.

"Bob and I had a long talk yesterday. At first, it was just about the break-in." She reached out and grabbed her cousin's hand. "Oh, Elaine, he was so upset. He kept circling the house checking and rechecking the windows and trying to figure out what, if anything, had been taken. I hated seeing him like that."

"That's terrible."

Jan nodded. "I think he was feeling a little violated, more than anything. Angry that someone felt they had the right to break into another person's home."

"I certainly understand."

"Me too."

The kettle whistled, and Jan got up to fetch it, along with two cups and the tea tin.

"So did he figure out for sure if anything was missing?"

"That's the strange part." Jan carried everything back to the table and Elaine immediately set about pouring their tea. "He said it doesn't look like anything is gone. Things were obviously disturbed, but nothing was missing. What do you make of that?"

Elaine shook her head and then took a sip of her tea. Blowing out a sigh that sounded like frustration, she set down her cup and drummed her fingers against the table. "I have got to get over to see Priscilla. Maybe she can shed some light on all of this."

"That's a good idea, but I'm afraid I can't go with you. Bob has been so worked up since his house was broken into that he insisted he come by this afternoon to check the locks on the tearoom." She glanced at the clock. "I actually expect him in about an hour. I can call him and ask him to come another time."

She started to rise, but Elaine motioned her back into her chair.

"That's all right. I'll give Nathan a call and see if he wants to come with me."

"Are you sure?" Jan asked. She knew that Elaine wasn't as close to Priscilla as she was, and it might be an awkward visit. But she was also sure that the two women were both kind and well meaning, and might just forge a close friendship of their own in time.

"Absolutely. Don't worry about it."

Jan nodded and sank slowly back into her seat.

"Now, back to your conversation with Bob." Elaine picked up her cup. "Did you talk about anything besides his home being broken into?"

Jan stared down into her tea. Elaine's casual tone didn't fool her. She knew exactly what information she was angling for, but just thinking about what they'd said made her heart hurt. She forced down the lump that rose in her throat. "Bob purchased his plane ticket."

She looked up. Elaine watched her, the same hurt Jan felt reflected in her eyes. She fidgeted with the handle of her cup. "When does he leave?"

"Two weeks. He promised he'd come back to Lancaster often and I said I would go to visit him in Baltimore, but the truth is…"

She broke off as the burning in her throat threatened to overwhelm her.

Elaine grasped her fingers. "Oh, Jan, I'm so sorry."

Jan took a moment to collect herself. When she could talk, she said, "Thank you. It's just…I have to admit my faith is a little bruised. I can't figure out why, after so many years of being a widow, God would bring someone into my life and let me fall in love with him, just to have him decide to go away."

Thankfully, Elaine didn't offer any of the platitudes that spoke to a person's head, but not her heart. She listened silently and conveyed love and compassion with a light touch or kind look. She even wiped tears from her own eyes when Jan spoke of her loneliness after Peter died. Jan loved her all the more for it.

Jan picked up a napkin and dried her eyes. "All right then, that's enough of that. You need to go see Priscilla, and I need to fix my face before Bob gets here. I'd rather he didn't know I've been crying."

Elaine rose and collected their empty teacups. "He's going to know you've been crying, and that's okay. He's as upset about leaving you as you are about him."

"Still, he doesn't need to see my red nose." Jan crossed to the cupboard and threw her napkin in the trash. "That's what powder is for."

She drew in a deep breath and blew it out through her mouth. "Thank you, Elaine."

Elaine dropped open the door to the dishwasher and set the teacups gently inside. "For what?"

Though she searched, Jan couldn't quite find the words to express what was in her heart. "For just being you," she whispered finally.

Elaine sniffed, obviously fighting tears of her own. "Yes, well, I'm as lucky as you in that department."

She enveloped Jan in a strong hug and then gave her a gentle push toward the door. "Now, get upstairs and powder your nose before Bob gets here."

Jan did as she was told and scurried up the stairs. It felt good to have someone to share her feelings with, someone to talk to and cry with.

It was just that she had hoped that someday, that someone might be Bob.

CHAPTER SEVEN

Despite the fact that she and Nathan had known each other since childhood, Elaine's heart still did a little pitter-pat when she saw him striding up their driveway in his neat khakis and polo shirt. Nathan wasn't a big man or overly muscled, but he kept in shape and it showed. Compared to him...

Elaine smoothed her hand over her navy polka-dot blouse and regretted the extra scone she'd had after lunch.

Appreciation gleamed in his eyes as he looked her over from head to toe. "You look nice."

Instantly, she felt better. She smiled. "Thank you. So do you."

He offered his elbow. "Are you ready to go?"

"I am."

Elaine slid her hand snugly on to his arm. This wasn't a date, but Nathan could make any occasion feel special with his tender, attentive manner. He opened her door and seated her inside his car, then circled around to the driver's side.

The ride to Priscilla's house was over too quickly in Elaine's opinion. She relished their long talks and quiet moments alone together—something she had missed terribly after Ben died.

Elaine had made sure to call before she and Nathan headed to the attractive little cottage Priscilla called home. It always reminded Elaine of a doll's house, with its delicate fretwork and pretty painted shutters. Nathan flipped on his blinker as they approached. The sun had set and dusk was settling quite heavily now, but a lamppost in Priscilla's front yard sent out a welcoming glow.

Elaine squinted as a pair of taillights glowed in front of them. A dark car backed out just before they pulled in. Elaine stiffened. It was difficult to tell in the dark, but the car could have been blue. She pointed her thumb over her shoulder in the direction the car had taken. "Did that car look dark blue to you?"

Nathan raised an eyebrow and peered into the rearview mirror. "The car that just left? I have no idea. I didn't get a good look at it."

Elaine nodded rapidly. "Pasha was driving a car like that. What do you suppose he was doing here?"

Nathan shook his head. "Well, there are lots of blue cars around. How do you know that one was Pasha's?"

Elaine reached for the buckle on her seat belt. "You're right. I don't. So let's go inside and find out." Her heels clattered on the brick walk as she hurried toward the house. "Shall we?"

Smiling, Nathan hurried to catch up.

They walked up the steps at a much slower pace and waited while he knocked. Priscilla opened the door, a happy smile on her face. *Why, she really is pretty*, Elaine thought, studying her through new and appreciative eyes. Though Priscilla always dressed conservatively, her trim figure was obvious in her sleek pencil skirt. Her hair was a warm chocolate brown, not mousy by any means, and she kept it neatly coiffed. And was that a glow adding color to her cheeks?

None of your business, Elaine, she chastised herself silently.

She stepped forward and pasted on a bright smile. "Hello, Priscilla. Thank you for seeing us on such short notice. I hope we're not keeping you from something."

Nathan turned his gaze to her, and Elaine wanted to kick herself.

"I mean, I know it's a Sunday night, and you probably have to get up early for work."

Priscilla laughed lightly and opened the door wide. "It's seven thirty, Elaine. I won't be ready for bed for hours."

Elaine's cheeks heated. It seemed she was determined to cast Priscilla in an old spinster's role. "Of c-course," she stammered.

She and Nathan stepped into the hall and Priscilla closed the door behind them. Much like the woman herself, Priscilla's home was warm and welcoming, but one would be hard pressed to miss her love of books. It was evident in the wallpaper border stamped with colorful books and in the framed pages from famous novels that lined the hallway.

"Would either of you like something to drink?" Priscilla gestured toward the kitchen. "I've got drinks and bottled water in the refrigerator, or if you'd prefer, Elaine, I can put a kettle on to boil for tea."

"Bottled water is fine for me," Elaine said.

Nathan agreed, and Priscilla led them to a small sitting room and then went to fetch their water.

Priscilla really did have exquisite taste. Elaine sighed with pleasure as she sank onto a deep red velvet couch—the kind one expected to find in a perfectly appointed parlor. Opposite was a beautiful Queen Anne rocking chair covered in the same fabric. Nathan chose there to sit. Priscilla returned a moment later, a bottle in each hand.

"Sorry about the mess." She handed them the water and then bent to scoop an array of pamphlets and flyers off the scrolled coffee table. "A friend of mine was just going over some home security systems with me. After the break-in, I thought I should look into having something installed." She glanced at Elaine. "Do you know Curtis Hanson?"

Yes, she knew Curtis. Though he was retired, he was only in his fifties, and he still helped out at the hardware store now and then.

"I'm glad you're looking into something," Elaine continued. "You must have been terribly upset after the break-in." She unscrewed the cap on her water and laid it on the coffee table. "Now that a couple of days have passed, have you had time to check if anything is missing?"

Priscilla shook her head and sat down on the couch next to Elaine. "It's the strangest thing, Elaine. It doesn't appear as though anything is gone. I don't own a lot of expensive jewelry, but what I do have is still in my jewelry chest on top of my dresser. Why do you suppose they didn't take it?"

"Maybe they didn't have time?" Nathan offered. "Depending on what time you got home, you may have scared them off."

Elaine smiled. "You were working late the night of the break-in, right?"

Priscilla nodded. "Yes, and thank goodness too. I don't know what I would have done if I'd been here alone." Her eyes filled with tears, which she blinked quickly away. "You know, I've never minded living alone, especially here in Lancaster. But now, for the first time..." She pointed to the stack of pamphlets she'd removed from the table. "Well, you see what it has come to. I no longer feel perfectly safe in my own house."

"I'm sure that will pass in time," Elaine urged softly.

"I hope you're right, but for now, I just feel like something precious has been taken from me, something that has nothing to do with material things. Isn't that funny? Nothing is missing, but everything is gone."

Elaine's heart ached at the grief she read on Priscilla's face. "I'm so sorry," she said, but knew even as she said the words that they weren't enough.

"Thank you," she replied.

"Do the police have any idea how the intruder got inside your house?"

Priscilla nodded. "The lock on the back door was jimmied. The police officer who took my statement said he could tell by the scratches the intruder left on the mechanism. That's one of the things Curtis recommended I change. He replaced the old lock I had with a deadbolt, but he still thought I should consider changing the old wood door to something a little sturdier. He offered to help me look for a steel door next week, something pretty but still functional."

"That's good," Elaine said.

Elaine took a drink of her water. "So what else can you tell us about the break-in? Besides nothing being taken, was there anything else you thought strange?"

Priscilla bit her lip. "Well, there were a couple of things, but like I told the police, it was just so silly."

Elaine's interest was instantly piqued. She leaned forward and realized as she did so that she was, literally, on the edge of her seat. "What was it, Priscilla? What did you see?"

"All of my closet doors were open. Also, there was . . . well, my suitcases from when I was gone. Oh, this is so ridiculous, I know. The intruder probably bumped them out of the way while they were looking around. Still, it was the only thing I noticed that appeared to have been disturbed. Isn't that strange?"

She looked from Elaine to Nathan. "I had them sitting by the laundry so I could empty out the clothes that needed to be washed. One of them had been knocked over. And that was it. That was the only thing I could see that looked at all out of place. I guess I scared them away before they could do any real damage. The intruders must have seen the glow from my headlights and rushed off."

Elaine agreed it was strange, but as Priscilla had suggested, more than likely the suitcase had been knocked over by accident when the intruder moved past them.

"What else is in the laundry room?" Nathan asked. "Anything important?"

"Just the circuit breaker box and the water heater." Priscilla lifted one hand questioningly. "Why the intruder would be rooting around in there, I have no idea."

"That is strange," Elaine agreed. She motioned toward the hall. "Would you mind if we took a look?"

Priscilla shrugged and stood. "Not at all. Right this way."

She led the way down the hall, past the kitchen to the laundry room.

"Sorry," Priscilla said as she reached for the knobs on the bi-fold doors. "It's an old house."

Elaine immediately knew what she meant once the doors were open. Like most old houses, this one had a vintage smell—like dust and damp mingled with mothballs.

Priscilla pointed toward a vent in the floor. "I think that's the source of the musty smell. At one time, there was an old wood-burning stove in the basement and the vent was to allow the heat from it to radiate upward. I keep meaning to hire somebody to close up the hole, but then I would have to replace the floor and I don't think I could get wood that matches the rest of the house anymore."

Elaine eyed the glowing oak with appreciation. "Your floors really are beautiful. I understand why you don't want to change them." She frowned and pointed to a deep scratch that wound under the door. "Has that always been there?"

Priscilla gasped and leaned closer. "No, it hasn't. I have no idea how it got there."

Nathan crouched and ran his finger along the gouge. "Looks like something pretty heavy was dragged across the floor."

"Your suitcase, maybe?" Elaine offered.

"Maybe. Although it is on wheels." Priscilla looked around in bewilderment. "But why? What could they have been looking for in here?"

Nathan stood and crossed to the circuit breaker box. Flipping open the cover, he examined each of the breakers. When he finished, he shut the door with a click. "Just checking."

Elaine snapped her fingers. "Of course! You thought they might have been messing with the circuits in case they intend to come back—like to keep the porch lights from coming on or something."

"You think they might come back?" Priscilla's eyes widened and her voice rose shrilly.

"I don't know," Elaine said.

"Well," Nathan said, "these circuits all look perfectly normal. I doubt they've been tampered with at all."

"I'm sorry, Priscilla," Elaine apologized hastily. "I didn't mean to scare you."

Priscilla blew out a breath and wrapped her arms around herself. "It's okay—I'm glad you checked. Just one more reason to get that security system installed."

Elaine agreed. They checked out the rest of the utility room from corner to corner, but found nothing unusual. When they finished, Elaine closed the doors with a sigh.

Priscilla's gaze bounced between her and Nathan as she fidgeted nervously. "I feel pretty foolish for telling the police about the closets and my suitcases."

Elaine gave a firm shake of her head. "We may not know what the intruders were looking for, but every detail, no matter how small or seemingly insignificant, is important. If they were out of place, then you were right to tell them."

She instantly looked relieved. "Thank you, Elaine."

"You're welcome. And now…" Elaine darted a quick glance at Nathan. They hadn't talked about telling Priscilla about the gun they'd found in the tearoom, but she had a right to know, especially if it was the same weapon used by the people behind break-ins. Elaine briefly summed up their discovery and how they'd managed to match the gun found by Jan to the article Elaine read earlier that day.

When she finished, Priscilla's eyes rounded in disbelief. "But if the gun you and Jan found is the same one used in the break-ins…" She shuddered and put her hand to her mouth. "Elaine, do you realize you probably talked to the person who broke into my house?"

Elaine nodded somberly. It sounded so much worse to hear it stated in that way. "Since the make of the gun was so unusual, we thought it might be wise to get a picture of it and send it to a gun expert that Archie knows. Unfortunately, it could be some time before we hear from him."

Priscilla straightened in her chair. "Do you still have the picture?"

Elaine nodded. "It's on my phone. Why?"

"May I see it?"

"Of course." Elaine rummaged in her purse and then produced her phone. "Here it is."

She pulled up the picture and turned it for Priscilla to see. Priscilla looked at it and shivered. "And to think I came so close to coming into contact with them." She rubbed her hands briskly over her arms.

"I'm just glad God was watching over you," Elaine said as she replaced her phone in her purse.

Priscilla nodded. "Me too."

The three of them spent a few more minutes chatting before Nathan indicated they should be going.

"Thanks again for your time, Priscilla." Elaine stood and gave her a quick hug. "And I'm glad you're looking into a home security system. I know I would feel better having something like that installed."

"Me too," Priscilla said. She bit her lip sadly. "I love our little town, but I worry that it might not ever feel quite the same for me."

Elaine felt her stomach drop. "I'm so sorry, Priscilla. You will give that feeling time to fade though, right? It could be that just having a security system will give you the peace of mind you need."

"Maybe," she replied, but her lips turned down doubtfully. She followed them to the door and walked with them out onto the porch. "Anyway, thanks for stopping by."

"You bet." Nathan's eyebrows rose and he pointed to the rather large fenced-in backyard behind Priscilla's house. "Say, you've got plenty of room back there. Ever thought about getting a dog?"

She smiled. "I've thought about it, but to be honest, I'm more of a cat person."

Elaine chuckled, thinking of Earl Grey. She dipped her head toward Priscilla. "So am I."

Nathan shrugged. "Well, it's just a thought. There's a pretty large shelter in Waterville if you change your mind."

Elaine laughed and grasped Priscilla's hand to give it a pat. "We'll be going now, but don't hesitate to call if you need anything."

"Thank you," she said. The squeeze she gave Elaine's fingers conveyed how much she appreciated the words.

"And I'll be praying that you get some of that peace back that has been missing too."

Priscilla's eyes welled and she nodded. "Thank you, Elaine," she whispered. Her gaze drifted over Elaine's shoulder and she lifted her hand in a wave. "Good night, Nathan."

"Good night," he said, then reached out his hand to guide Elaine down the stairs. Once they were back in the car, he waited until she buckled her seat belt into place before lifting his eyebrows questioningly. "So? What did you think?"

Though she knew what he meant, Elaine couldn't help but tease. She hid a smile as she turned in the seat to look at him. "I think you were absolutely right."

Nathan eyed her curiously as he inserted the key into the ignition. "Oh yeah?"

She nodded.

"About what?"

Elaine quirked an eyebrow, but it didn't last. She couldn't help but laugh. "Priscilla's yard *is* big enough for a dog."

CHAPTER EIGHT

Jan checked her face in the mirror one last time before heading down the stairs to meet Bob, whose silver Acura was just now easing slowly up the driveway. She laid her hand on the doorknob and took a deep breath before throwing the door open wide.

"Steady, girl," she murmured to herself as he stepped from the car.

Jan had always found Bob attractive. He was handsome and distinguished looking, but he had a boyish charm. Still, he was strong and sensible. Steady. Someone to cling to.

Her heart thumped painfully but she lifted her chin and offered a bright smile as he swung up the porch steps.

"Hi." Bob's warm gaze held hers.

He was searching for something, Jan knew. She looked away, unable to endure the hopeful gleam she read in his eyes.

She swallowed the heavy knot in her throat. "Hi, Bob."

She stepped back into the hallway to let him pass and then closed the door behind him before motioning toward the kitchen. "I'm making some tea. Would you like some?"

Disappointment flickered on his face. He slid his hands into the pockets of his beige trousers, and for a moment Jan thought he might decline. Instead, his features relaxed and he offered a sad sort of smile.

"I'd love some. Thanks." He extended his hand toward the kitchen. "Shall we?"

Nervousness fluttered in Jan's stomach as she passed him and led the way into the kitchen, which was silly really, since she and Bob were long past this stage. Still, she couldn't help the tremor that shook her fingers as she reached for two teacups and set them on the table.

"The water is just about ready." She gestured with her chin over her shoulder. "Go ahead and have a seat."

Her brave act wasn't fooling Bob. She felt him watching her as she withdrew a plate of lemons from the refrigerator to set alongside the cream and sugar bowl.

"Jan? Are you okay?"

She kept her back to him and blinked away a sudden swell of tears. Honestly, she'd not felt such a jumble of emotions since she'd lost Peter. It wasn't pleasant.

Sighing, she turned back to the table, set down the lemons, and pulled out a chair. "I guess we should talk."

Bob—who had seemed so strong just a moment before—let his shoulders slump. He nodded. "I guess so."

Jan slid into the chair and clasped her hands tightly in her lap. "Nothing has changed. I can't go with you, Bob. My home is here."

"I know."

"The tearoom is really taking off. I can't leave Elaine to manage it all by herself. And I love it. It's my dream. You know all this."

"I know," he repeated.

A tremor seized her voice. "Besides, what would my kids say if I just up and left? You remember how long it took Brian to accept this new business venture. He was so worried that I was throwing away my life's savings. If I let all of it go now he'll worry that he was right all along and…"

Bob reached under the table and took hold of one of her hands. "Jan."

She stared at him, her throat tight.

"It's okay. I admit, I was hoping…but I never really expected that you would change your mind about marrying me. I know how much this place means to you."

Neither of them spoke for a second, both of them letting the normal, everyday sounds of the old house fill the silence until they could find their voices.

"I'm really sorry, Bob," Jan whispered finally. "I know how important this move is to you."

"It is," he agreed. "It's the chance of a lifetime."

Somehow, hearing the words again solidified Jan's resolve. She squeezed Bob's fingers and then pulled her hand away.

"You're going to love living in Baltimore," she said, trying to be positive. She rose to get the kettle.

"I think so. It may take some time to settle in, but I'll have my work to keep me busy," Bob said. "Being a partner means I'll have extra responsibility, but that will be good right at first. It'll help me keep my focus, and not concentrate on how much I miss you."

Jan smiled lovingly. "I'm hoping for the same thing over here."

He continued to talk about the job as Jan poured the tea. She set a cup in front of him and then wrapped her fingers around the second cup, glad for the warmth that radiated through the china into her fingers. Slowly, excitement replaced the sorrow in his voice as he talked about the cases that already awaited him in Baltimore. Though her heart was heavy, Jan couldn't help but smile at the enthusiasm in his voice as he chattered on about how nice it would be to tackle the philanthropic cases he would now take on. She sipped her tea quietly while he spoke, nodding every now and then to hide the fact that every word pierced like a sliver in her heart.

"What about your house here?" she asked when he finished. "Are you going to try and close it up before you leave?"

She read the hesitation on his face and tensed.

He lowered his gaze, and his long fingers smoothed the edges of a napkin. "Actually, Jan, I was thinking about renting it."

"Won't that be difficult with you living so far away?"

"Not if I do it through a Realtor." He looked around the kitchen. "I was hoping you might be able to recommend someone. Maybe the person who helped you and Elaine find this place?"

Jan's heart felt frozen inside her chest. If Bob rented his house—the house he'd lived in for more than twenty years— he wasn't planning on coming back to Lancaster soon.

She swallowed...or tried to. Her dry throat made it almost impossible. "I didn't realize you were thinking of renting."

He fidgeted uncomfortably with the handle on his teacup. "Well, I wasn't at first, but now that the move is here, I feel it makes sense. I'll be tempted to keep looking over my shoulder otherwise and…wondering."

Afraid of what she'd see in his eyes, she focused on the gold rim of her cup. "I suppose that's true, except, well, are you sure? What if you change your mind about Baltimore?"

She waited, each passing second measured by the thumping of her heart. She heard his clothing rustle and then he reached out and took her hand.

"I won't change my mind, Jan," he said at last. "But despite everything, I'm still hoping you will."

For a split second, joy fluttered like birds inside Jan's chest.

"I'm n-not sure I understand," she said carefully.

Bob's grip tightened. "I'm asking you to marry me, Jan. Again."

The fluttering in Jan's chest became full-fledged panic. "Bob, wait. We've talked about this."

"I know I'm asking a lot of you, considering all the changes in your life recently. A move like this is probably more than you bargained for when you agreed to go out with me that first time." His voice grew hoarse, his gaze more earnest. "But I love you, Jan. The only thing that could make this trip more perfect is to have you with me when I go to Baltimore. All I'm asking for is a chance to make you happy, to build a life for the two us like the one you had with Peter. Will you let me try?"

Jan had never been more thankful to be seated. Her knees trembled, her hands shook, and her insides felt like Jell-O. Why, oh why, couldn't she have met Bob sooner, before she and Elaine went into business together? Before she'd fallen in love with this house and her new life in Lancaster?

A flush colored Bob's cheeks. "Jan?" He lifted his chin. "You've made up your mind, haven't you?"

She couldn't lie, and didn't want to. She gave a slow nod.

"And you're not coming with me."

It wasn't a question. She dropped her gaze.

"I figured as much."

There was a hitch in his voice that hadn't been there before. Jan met his eyes. "I'm sorry, Bob."

He gave a sad sort of shrug that tore her heart. "Don't be." He reached into his pocket and pulled out a sheet of paper.

Jan stared at it curiously. "What is that?"

"My itinerary. I changed my ticket. I figured there was no sense prolonging my departure. I leave next week."

Jan's stomach sank. So he really hadn't believed she would change her mind, but he'd come to ask anyway. She swallowed hard. "Next week? But what about your house?"

"I'll rent it fully furnished so there's no hurry to move my stuff. The house will probably show better if it looks lived in anyway. And I've arranged for a friend to keep up with the yard, cleaning, all of it, until I get a renter. Hopefully, it won't be long."

"Next week," Jan repeated. "That's really soon."

The hurt in his eyes broke her heart. She rubbed her palms over her eyes, not caring if she smudged her mascara, or if her nose looked red.

"I love you, Jan." He didn't touch her, just sat looking at her for what seemed like an eternity. Finally, he rose and turned away, his long strides carrying him swiftly out of the kitchen.

A moment later Jan heard his car start, then he was gone. And he'd forgotten to check their locks.

CHAPTER NINE

Monday passed in a blur for Jan. Thankfully, business was good and she stayed too busy to think much about the look on Bob's face after she told him she hadn't changed her mind about marrying him and moving with him to Baltimore. Now that the tearoom was closed, however, she felt the stab of longing afresh.

Elaine eyed her over the stack of dishes Jan was loading into the dishwasher. "Are you all right? You've seemed a little out of sorts all day."

"I'm fine," Jan lied, and immediately felt contrite. She dried her hands on a dish towel and then punched the start button on the dishwasher. "Actually, I'm not fine. Bob's moving has me in knots."

Elaine nodded in sympathy. "I imagine. How did it go yesterday? Did you have a chance to talk?"

Jan debated about telling her of Bob's second marriage proposal, but knew if she did she'd be awash in tears all over again. Instead she gave a wave of her hand and then motioned toward Elaine. "What about you? How did it go with Priscilla?"

Jan was thankful that Elaine accepted her cue to change the subject. Elaine relayed the details of their visit and then eyed Jan quizzically. "I just can't figure it out, Jan. What do you suppose the people who broke into her home were after?"

"I don't know." Jan absentmindedly flipped off lights as she pondered the things Priscilla had said. "It's certainly strange."

"And Bob still hasn't found anything missing?"

"Nothing missing there either so far. But speaking of Bob's place..." Jan cleared her throat and lowered her gaze. "Do you happen to have the contact information for the Realtor we used when we bought the tearoom?"

"I'm sure I do somewhere. Probably in the office." Elaine lifted her eyebrows curiously. "Why?"

"Bob is going to need it. He's thinking about putting his house up for rent before he leaves for Baltimore."

She said the words quickly, before they could lodge in her throat and form an uncomfortable knot.

"You know," she continued hastily, "I'm kind of thinking about heading over to the Northwoods Bed-and-Breakfast. I'd like to see if I can find out anymore on that Philpott guy who was here in the tearoom the day we found the gun."

Elaine gave her a look that said she wasn't fooled by the sudden change of subject. Jan pretended not to notice and gathered up the soiled dish towels that needed to be laundered before they opened tomorrow.

"I mean, you've already gone to speak to that Jagr fellow and Priscilla," she continued as she deposited the towels into the laundry bin. "The least I can do is see what I can learn about Henry Philpott, don't you think?"

"I think that's a wonderful idea. Would you like me to come with you?"

Jan hesitated a moment, then shook her head. She needed time to think, something she could do better on her own. "No, thank you. But if you could find that Realtor's number for me while I'm gone, I would sure appreciate it."

"Will do." Elaine picked up a dishcloth and began wiping down the countertops. "I'll finish up in here. You go on and let me know what you find out."

Jan untied her apron strings thankfully. Elaine was not only her cousin, she was the best type of friend—the kind who knew when *not* asking questions was the best act of thoughtfulness one could give.

Jan grabbed her purse from the closet and took out her keys. "I'll be back soon. This will just be a quick visit, I'm sure."

"Take your time," Elaine said gently. "I'll order dinner while you're gone too. That way neither of us will have to cook when you get back. Does a burger from the Pine Tree Grill sound okay?"

"Sounds wonderful. Thank you, Elaine."

"No problem. Say hello to Ned and Rue for me."

"Will do." Jan tossed her a grateful glance and then hurried out the door.

The Northwoods Bed-and-Breakfast wasn't far from the tearoom, and the weather was much warmer than it had been just a couple of days earlier. Jan was tempted to walk, except that doing so meant she would have to be conscious of the time if she didn't want to walk home after dark.

She reluctantly turned for her Toyota and made the short drive in just a few minutes. In fact, finding a place to park took longer than the drive itself. Labor Day vacationers intent on squeezing out one last bit of summer packed the mini-golf course in the backyard of the rambling old farmhouse, but as far as Jan could tell, Henry Philpott wasn't one of them. She clutched her purse and climbed out of her car. After hitting the lock button, she turned up the sidewalk and went inside.

Rue Maxwell was a pretty woman, with soft blonde hair that she kept pinned up when she was working. She smiled as Jan entered and offered a quick wave before returning her attention to her customers—an elderly couple who were perusing a display of pamphlets and picking out sightseeing destinations with Rue's help.

While Rue chatted, Jan wandered around the farmhouse. Like the tearoom, it was elegantly appointed with a variety of antiques, yet still maintained its cozy feel. From the living room, a short hall led to the remodeled kitchen and dining room, both of which Jan had seen. She was glad Ned and Rue had been careful to keep the feel of the old house when they remodeled, so that even though the appliances and fixtures were new, they did not detract from the beauty of the place. Even the furniture seemed to fit, as though the wingback chairs by the bay window had always sat just so, and the chandelier hanging above the piano had always cast its cheery, sparkling light. In fact...

Jan moved closer to the piano, where the corner of a sheet of paper peeked out from under the piano bench. Sheet music, perhaps?

She grasped the corner and slid the paper out. When she flipped it over, she was surprised to see that the paper was not sheet music at all. It was a map.

"Hey, Jan. Sorry to keep you waiting." Rue strolled into the living room and poked her thumb over her shoulder. "I was helping a couple of our guests."

Jan adjusted her glasses. "Hi, Rue. No problem. I'm not keeping you from anything, am I?"

"Not at all. We're all finished." Rue glanced at the paper in Jan's hands. "What have you got there?"

She turned the page around for Rue to see. "It looks like a map." She pointed toward the piano bench. "I found it on the floor down there. Does it belong to you?"

Rue frowned and squinted while she looked over the map. "Not mine." She put her hand to her mouth and called over her shoulder. "Hey, hon?"

Ned poked his head out from the kitchen.

Rue gestured toward the paper in Jan's hand. "Did you lose a map?"

His eyebrows bunched as he frowned. "A map? Why would I have a map?"

Rue chuckled and waved her hand. "Never mind."

Ned ducked back into the kitchen and Rue snapped her fingers. "Hey, you know what? I bet this belongs to one of our guests. He was carrying around a bunch of them earlier this afternoon."

Jan's heart skipped a beat. "A guest? You wouldn't by any chance mean Henry Philpott?"

Rue's eyebrows rose in surprise. "Why, yes. Do you know Henry?"

"Not really," she admitted. "He came into the tearoom the other day, but I didn't actually get a chance to speak with him." She didn't mention that it was because he'd taken a sudden aversion to conversation the minute she'd started asking questions. Jan motioned toward the staircase. "Is he here?"

Rue shook her head. "He stepped out shortly after lunch. He seems like a nice enough fella, but he sure doesn't talk much."

"I noticed that too." Jan handed the map back to Rue. "But he did ask me about cottage rentals because most of the ones along the lake were booked. I pointed him here."

Rue's eyes widened appreciatively. "You did? That was sweet of you. Thanks, Jan." She motioned toward the kitchen. "Would you like something to drink?"

"No, I'm fine, thank you." Jan indicated the sofa with one hand. "Do you have a moment to talk? I can come back later if this isn't a good time."

"Of course I have time." Rue laughed, a lighthearted sound that made Jan smile. "You know me. I always have time to chat."

She led Jan over to the sofa. When they were seated, she gave her knee a pat. "Now, what can I do for you?"

Jan debated whether she should tell Rue about the gun she and Elaine had found in the tearoom, then decided against it. While it was interesting, and would explain Jan's interest in Henry Philpott, she didn't want to cause any gossip that might interfere with the investigation.

She set her purse on the cushion next to her while she weighed her words. "Rue, I hope you don't mind that I recommended your place to Mr. Philpott."

She raised her eyebrows as though startled. "Mind? Why would I mind? Referrals are good for business."

"Yes, I know, but I kind of got the impression when he was in the tearoom that he is a bit more unusual than your average guest."

Rue put her finger to her chin as though thinking. "I suppose you could say that. He does come and go a lot, and often at odd times of the day, but I just figure he's been sightseeing, or possibly puttering around checking out the things to do in Lancaster. I mean, why else would he have all those maps with him all of the time, right?"

Why, indeed? Jan bit her lip, thinking. "Rue, do you happen to know how long Mr. Philpott plans on staying in Lancaster?"

Rue's gaze appeared shuttered. "You mean how long he's booked his reservation?" She gave a slight shake of her head. "I, um, I really couldn't say."

"You mean he didn't tell you?"

"No, I mean I couldn't say." She grimaced. "I'm sorry, Jan. I trust you, but you know that Ned and I try and keep our guests' information confidential. I probably shouldn't even have told you what I did about his maps."

She looked truly worried now, as though her friendship with Jan had made her careless and she was just now realizing it.

"No need to apologize," Jan said quickly. "You and Ned take such good care of your guests. I should have realized you would want to protect their privacy too."

Rue immediately looked relieved. "Thank you, Jan."

Though she could hardly wait to get back to tell Elaine about the maps, Jan knew it would be rude to hurry off, so she stayed and chatted for almost an hour, until another customer came in and Rue was forced to cut their conversation short to wait on him.

"I suppose I should be getting back to work," Rue said, rising. "But if you'd like to wait…"

Jan cut her off with a shake of her head. "You've been very gracious, and I've taken up enough of your time already. Thank you so much, Rue."

Rue smiled and sent her off with a wave. Jan hurried to her car. Visiting with Rue had been nice, but she couldn't wait to return to the tearoom so she could relay everything she'd learned to Elaine.

CHAPTER TEN

Elaine lounged in the sitting room, flipping through the pages of a book without actually reading the words. She heard the kitchen door close and then Jan's muffled footsteps on the stairs. She set aside her book, eager to hear what Jan had learned about Henry Philpott.

"Jan, is that you?" she called out.

"It's me." Jan poked her head into the sitting room, her face flushed and her eyes bright.

Elaine took one glance at her cousin's face and nodded. "You were right," she said, without waiting for an explanation.

Jan hurried into the room and set her purse and sweater aside. "I was indeed. Henry Philpott *is* a guest at Ned and Rue's place. I guess he took me up on my suggestion after all."

Elaine clasped her hands tightly in her lap. "Any idea how long he's staying?"

Jan sank onto a chair. "Unfortunately, no. I asked, but Rue said she and Ned have a policy about sharing that sort of information about their guests."

Elaine pinched her bottom lip, thinking. "Yes, that makes sense. So then, what were you able to find out?"

Jan leaned forward, a gleam returned to her eyes. "Well, Rue was helping one of her guests when I arrived. While I was waiting for her to finish up, I went into the living room and happened upon a map that Rue said must have belonged to Mr. Philpott."

Elaine frowned. "What sort of map?"

"The topographical kind. You know, one that illustrates the physical characteristics of an area. This one was definitely of Lancaster. I recognized the lake right away."

Excitement built in Elaine's chest. "That is interesting. Why do you suppose he had it?"

"No idea, but Rue said he carries around a lot of them, not just that one. And he comes and goes at all hours of the day."

"Carries maps of Lancaster, comes and goes at odd hours, doesn't like answering questions." Elaine ticked the items off on her fingers and gave them a wiggle. "Three strikes?"

"Possibly. It certainly sounded suspicious to me." She scooted forward to grasp the arms of her chair. "Elaine, do you suppose Henry Philpott is using those maps of Lancaster to figure out which homes he's going to target?"

"I'm not sure about the geographical map, but the other maps maybe. Why else would he have them?"

"So then, there must some kind of order to the break-ins."

Elaine scrambled to her feet. "You're right. I think I have some old Rand McNallys around here someplace."

Jan snapped her fingers. "The office. I saw them when I was cleaning out the file cabinet. I'll get them."

While she waited for Jan to bring the atlases, Elaine cleared off the coffee table, then went to her room for a highlighter. Jan appeared a moment later.

"Well, I have them, but I don't think they're going to help much. They're state road maps. I doubt they'll have anything on Lancaster." She dropped the bound collection of maps on the table and held up something else with a smile. "This, on the other hand, should have everything we need."

Elaine plucked it from her hand. "A map of Lancaster? Where did this come from?"

"A couple of our tourist customers left it months ago. I kept it in case they came back for it. When they didn't, I forgot all about it."

"It's perfect." Elaine spread the map on the coffee table and pulled up a chair. Yanking the cap off of the highlighter, she leaned over the map. "Okay. Let's start by highlighting the streets where the break-ins have occurred."

While she perused the map, Jan drew up a chair next to hers. "There's Bob's street." She pointed at a spot on the map.

"Good." Elaine traced Bob's street with the highlighter. She moved her hand down the map. "And here is Priscilla's house." She traced the length of Priscilla's street and then frowned. "That's pretty far from Bob's." Elaine tapped the map with the highlighter, and then frowned. "Well, apart from two yellow lines, what have we got?"

"Maybe there's a connection." Jan sat back, thinking. "That newspaper article where we first read about the break-ins—did it happen to mention where the others took place?"

Elaine shook her head. "I don't think so. Not that I remember anyway."

"Me either. But I bet I know someone who could tell us."

"Candace, over at the *Penzance Courier*?"

Jan nodded and rose. "I'll call her."

Fortunately, Candace was in the office. Jan chatted with her for several minutes and took down notes. When she hung up, she carried the paper back to Elaine. "Here you go. Candace said there have been five break-ins in all, and she didn't believe they were actually related."

Elaine studied the two remaining streets. "Did she say if anything was taken?"

"Some houses, yes, some no. The odd thing is the missing items all are so random—jewelry, an old clock, a few trinkets."

"So they're not after valuables."

"It wouldn't appear so."

Elaine frowned. "Could it be they are just taking things to throw the police off their track?"

They both pondered that idea.

Elaine handed Jan the paper and took out her highlighter. "Anyway, let's go ahead and finish highlighting the streets that have already been hit. Will you read me the other addresses?"

"Sure." Jan adjusted her glasses and read the first name. "Ready? The first is 81 Oak Lane. Right there."

Elaine added another highlighted line. "Next?"

"It's 8128 Crosstimber."

Elaine searched a minute and then found the street. "Whose house is that?"

Jan shrugged. "No idea." She bent over the list and read the next street. "I don't know whose house this is either. It's 8176 Cleveland Drive."

Instead of highlighting the street, Elaine paused.

Jan's brows rose. "Elaine? Everything all right?"

Elaine's heart rate sped up as an idea struck. "Jan, do you notice anything strange about these addresses?"

Jan's gaze dropped to the paper in her hands. After a second, Elaine took the paper and added Bob's address and Priscilla's, then handed it back.

Suddenly, Jan's eyes widened. "They all start with eight and one."

Elaine nodded in excitement. "Priscilla's is 811 Danbury. And Bob's starts with 81 too."

Jan shook her head. "What does it mean? Why would anyone be targeting houses with those numbers in the address?"

"I don't know, but I think it's worth mentioning to Dan."

"Me too," Jan said.

The cousins fell silent, thinking. Finally, Elaine sighed and rubbed her hand over her face.

"So we've got Philpott and Jagr we're suspicious of, but we don't even know why yet. Even if one or the other is guilty, we still don't know why they'd break into people's homes to steal trinkets. It just doesn't make any sense."

"No, it doesn't." The frustration in Jan's sigh matched Elaine's.

Elaine propped her hands on her knees and lifted her chin. "Well, we have to do something, don't you think? Someone is destroying the peace and safety we love about Lancaster, and I for one intend to do something about it."

She waited while Jan's emotions registered on her face—hesitation, concern, and finally determination.

She took a deep breath and squared her shoulders. "You're right, Elaine. We can't sit by while our friends are targeted. So?" She crossed her arms and her head tipped at a jaunty angle. "What do you say we catch us a thief?"

CHAPTER ELEVEN

Now that the Labor Day holiday was over, business at the tearoom had returned to a more normal, steady pace on Tuesday, and would probably stay so today too. The Wednesday crowd usually consisted of many of their regulars, with only a few tourists mingled in. It would be a calm and manageable day.

Elaine put the finishing touches on a new napkin fold she was trying, then stepped back to examine her handiwork.

Nice.

But time consuming.

She sighed.

"What's that?" Jan bustled past Elaine carrying a tray of sugar bowls to place on the tables.

"It's a napkin rose. I saw it on one of those craft Web sites and thought we could use it here in the tearoom."

Jan put down her tray and examined the intricately folded napkin. "It's beautiful, Elaine."

Elaine touched the rose with the tip of her finger. "But not very practical. This one took me almost twenty minutes to get right. At that rate, it would take me a week to make enough for the entire tearoom."

"*Hmm.*" Jan chuckled. "Well, maybe we could just fold up a few for special occasions."

"Now that idea, I like." Elaine smiled and moved to the tray to help with the sugar bowls. As she picked one up, she eyed her cousin curiously. "So? Have you given any more thought to our 'friends'?"

"Jagr and Philpott?"

Elaine smiled conspiratorially. "You thinking what I'm thinking?"

"Uh-huh. Maybe after the tearoom closes today…"

The bell over the front door rang, and both Elaine and Jan looked up to see a young woman sporting a thick blonde braid enter. She was an attractive girl, with the lithe figure that dancers often possessed. But it was her striking blue eyes that arrested Elaine's attention.

Jan looked down at her watch and then at the young woman. "Oh dear, I'd better go and tell her that we're not quite ready to open."

"Jan, wait." Elaine grabbed her hand before she could move away. "Don't you recognize her?"

"Should I?" Jan watched the woman discreetly over Elaine's shoulder. "She doesn't look familiar."

Elaine cupped one hand over her mouth. "She's the woman I told you about from the day we discovered the gun in the tearoom. Remember? She was arguing with that young man—Matthew, I think his name was—and left here in tears."

"You mean Irina?" Jan's eyes widened and she tilted her head to get a better peek around Elaine. "Are you sure?"

"Positive." Elaine brushed the sugar off her hands and then shot a warning glance at Jan. "I'm going to go see what she wants."

"If her actions are anything to go by, it appears she's looking for something."

Elaine blinked in confusion. "What?"

Jan gave a thrust of her chin. "See for yourself."

Elaine turned quietly. Irina did indeed appear to be searching for something as she moved in and out among the tables, her shoulders hunched and her gaze fixed to the carpet.

"Jan," Elaine, whispered, her heart pounding hard inside her chest, "do you think she might be looking for the gun?"

"It's possible," Jan whispered back. She clutched Elaine's hand, her eyes wide and fearful. "Maybe you shouldn't go over there."

Elaine straightened. "Nonsense. I'll just keep getting the tables ready while I work my way toward her. Maybe I'll be able to figure out what she's doing here."

"And if not?"

Elaine shrugged coyly. "I'll ask her if she wants some tea."

Jan gave a hopeless shake of her head, but Elaine merely smiled as she picked up two more bowls. She carried one toward a table near the center of the room, mindful as she walked not to draw Irina's attention. Not that she need have worried. The woman seemed particularly preoccupied as she circled the table where she and Matthew had sat together just a few days ago.

And she was holding a phone to her ear, Elaine noted, as Irina pulled out a chair with one hand, looked under the table, and then pushed it back. Who was she talking to?

Carrying the glass bowl, Elaine sidled closer. Irina definitely seemed agitated. Her loose hand fluttered while she talked and her booted heels thumped rapidly across the carpeted floor.

Suddenly, she straightened and Elaine froze in her tracks.

"I said I'm sure!" Irina snapped, her voice angry and harsh—and strangely devoid of the strong accent Elaine remembered. "I've looked everywhere. I don't see anything."

She kept her back to Elaine, listening to the person on the other end of the line. One hand gripped the top of a chair, and Elaine couldn't help but notice the taut skin over her knuckles. Her tight grip was rapidly turning her flesh white.

"I could ask them, I suppose, but more than likely we're out of luck."

With the last few words, Irina turned and caught sight of Elaine standing just a few feet away. Her blue eyes narrowed and Elaine felt herself literally gulp. She set down the sugar bowl and clasped both hands in front of her.

"Can I help you?" she asked feebly.

Irina cupped her phone close to her lips. "I'll call you back."

She immediately clicked off and shoved her phone into the pocket of her tight blue jeans. "Are you the owner?"

Now that she was speaking directly to her, Elaine was certain she'd been correct about Irina's accent. It had not just faded, it was wholly and completely gone.

Elaine tried not to let the knowledge show as she nodded. "I'm the co-owner. My cousin Jan and I are in business together."

Irina seemed to ponder this a moment and then nodded. "My friend and I were in here the other day." She paused to glance around the tearoom. "You have a nice place."

"Thank you."

She dipped her head. "Listen, I don't suppose you have a lost and found, do you?"

So she *was* searching for something. Excitement built inside Elaine, making her hands tremble. She laced her fingers behind her back. "No, I'm sorry, we don't. Did you lose something?"

Irina seemed to measure Elaine for several long seconds. "This is going to sound a little odd, I suppose. It's just that my friend and I..."

The back door slammed and a loud crash cut her off before she could finish. Elaine whirled to look for Jan. She stood frozen, her features showing she was as startled as Elaine felt.

"What was that?" Jan asked.

"No idea."

Irina forgotten, Elaine hurried out of the parlor and down the hall with Jan at her heels. As they neared the kitchen, she spotted Archie's long legs poking out from behind the table. Thankfully, they were moving.

Elaine circled the table. "Archie? Are you all right?"

Archie gave a low groan and pushed out from under a large cardboard box. "I think so."

Jan hurried to help him move the box away. "What happened?" She grunted as she gave the box a tug. "And what on earth is in this box?"

"Magazines," Archie said, grumbling as he rubbed the top of his head and stood. "Art magazines, to be exact. I picked them up from a used book store in Waterville."

Elaine peeled back one of the flaps. "There certainly are a lot of them in there. They nearly tore a whole right through the bottom of this box."

"I know. I do believe that's why I lost my balance and fell."

"You didn't hit your head, did you?" Jan asked, frowning at him in concern. "You look a little pale."

"A bit, but it's not bad. Bruised mostly." He grimaced and prodded his scalp gingerly. "Like my ego."

"Poor Archie." Elaine *tsked* softly. "I'll get you an ice pack."

"No need, though I may require an aspirin later." Archie threw a glance toward the door. "Who were you talking to in there? I thought I heard someone up front, but it's too early for customers."

Both Elaine and Jan gave a simultaneous gasp and then Elaine hurried back toward the west parlor, where she'd left Irina. The woman had been about to tell her what she was searching for when Archie arrived. Maybe if she caught her in time, she still would.

Elaine burst into the parlor, not bothering to compose herself the way she had when Irina first appeared. If she looked flustered, she could easily say it was because of Archie's fall. She scanned the back corner of the parlor where Irina had been standing when the crash occurred. Nothing.

Maybe she'd gone across the hall to continue her search. Elaine hurried into the east parlor. It also was empty. She was too late.

Irina was gone.

Elaine stifled a growl of frustration. The woman was gone, and so was her chance to find out what Irina had been looking for. On the off chance she could still catch her, Elaine hurried to the door and glanced out upon an empty driveway. Why had Irina left in such a hurry?

Jan skittered into the parlor. "Is she...?"

"Too late," Elaine said. "She must have gone out the front door when we rushed to check on Archie."

"Who did?" The color had returned to Archie's cheeks and he actually looked a tad curious as he followed Jan into the parlor. "What have I missed?"

"Irina," Elaine explained. "She was here when you came in and she appeared to be looking for something."

"The woman with the Russian-sounding accent?"

"That's the one," she said. But then she froze. "But you wouldn't have thought so today."

Archie gave a perplexed frown. "What do you mean?"

"She spoke perfect English, with not a trace of an accent."

CHAPTER TWELVE

Jan's hand rose to her chin. "No accent? Are you certain? Maybe it just sounded a little different without all of the chatter going on in the background."

Archie nodded in agreement. "There was a host of people in the tearoom that day."

Elaine shook her head adamantly. "I'm certain. The accent Irina used today was nothing like what I heard on Saturday."

"So she was faking?" Disbelief soaked Jan's gaze. "Why would she do that? What did she have to gain?"

"Do you suppose it was some kind of joke?" Archie asked. "I've heard people do that from time to time."

Elaine thought a moment and then shook her head. "I've heard of people doing that too, but Irina and Matthew were arguing, remember? She left in tears. That doesn't sound like joking to me."

"Me neither." Jan's gaze bounced from Elaine to Archie. "What do you think? Is this something we should report to Dan?"

Elaine looked to Archie for help.

He rubbed his chin thoughtfully. "The lack of an accent is definitely odd, but is that alone enough to be considered suspicious? And her actions really don't tell us much. After all, she might easily have been looking for a sweater."

"That is true, but we have more we need to report to the trooper." Elaine explained what they'd discovered about the addresses and then paced the floor, her feet scuffing quietly against the carpet.

Archie's eyes gleamed with curiosity. "That is interesting news."

"As for Irina, I'm not sure we should say anything," Elaine said. "She didn't sneak in, after all. And she admitted she was looking for something. She asked about a lost and found." She stopped and raised her hands, palms up. "That doesn't sound like something a person with something to hide would do."

The worried lines on Jan's brow faded. "You're right, both of you. Irina might not know anything about the gun we found. Not everyone who comes in is suspect." She paused and then her jaw firmed and a look of determination entered her gaze. "But I still think we should find out more about her."

Elaine moved to one of the nearest tables and sat. "I agree. However, I think we will need to go about it a different way, and we'll need to look at all of the suspects, not just Irina."

Archie and Jan joined her at the table. Elaine motioned to Jan. "You're really good at sorting these things out. Maybe we should go back to the list of people in the tearoom that morning and start writing down the things we've learned about each one so we can keep track."

"I agree. I'll get started as soon our morning rush is over." She looked up at the clock above the fireplace. "Speaking of which, I'd best get back to the kitchen. We have only half an hour before we open." She turned to Elaine. "Will you call Dan?"

"Will do," Elaine said. "And after I've spoken to him, Archie and I will finish getting ready in here."

"What about Rose?" Archie asked.

Elaine looked at her watch. "She should be arriving any minute. In fact, I think I hear her now."

The low drone of a boat motor proved her assumption. Elaine made the call to Dan and then began the task of opening the tearoom—things that by now had become second nature. Jan wrote the cookie of the day on a small chalkboard while Elaine filled the cash drawer and turned on lights. A few minutes later, Rose joined them with a load of freshly washed and pressed linens that she stacked carefully in the china hutch to keep them from wrinkling. Archie swept the porch and brought in the newspaper before going to lift the shades and open the drapes.

"So tell me about the art magazines," Elaine said as she moved to help him. "You said you found them at a used bookstore in Waterville?"

Archie nodded as he smoothed his hand over the heavy silk fabric, arranging the drapes so they hung just so. "I got the idea after talking with Nathan. He recommended a place I could go to have my father's painting authenticated."

"Yes, he told me. It's the same place in New York that Heather Wells recommended to me."

"Exactly so. Well, that started me thinking. I went online to see what procedures were involved in the process of authenticating an artist's work and discovered there were some trends I might be able pinpoint in my father's work. Trouble is, I don't have many pieces to compare it to, so I bought up those magazines hoping I might find some."

"Good idea."

"Yes, well, we'll see, I suppose. I've got a lot of searching ahead of me—which I fully intend to do on my off hours and at lunch."

Elaine laughed as she crossed to the front door. "Oh, Archie, we're not the least bit worried about that. In fact, if you'll leave a few of those magazines with me, I'll help you look." She arched an eyebrow. "So long as you tell me what I'm looking for."

"You have a deal."

Elaine chuckled and flipped the sign on the front door. A few moments later their first customers arrived, and all conversation revolved around work until the usual lunchtime lull. Because she had a test coming up in her culinary school, Rose took the first lunch break so she could wolf down a sandwich and study. Archie and Elaine pored over the art magazines.

Elaine pointed to a picture in one of the magazines. Like the painting done by Archie's father, it depicted a young woman. "What about this one?"

Archie shook his head. "The woman is in profile but the colors aren't quite right."

Elaine frowned. "Tell me again what we're looking for."

"Stylistic similarities," Archie said. He took a moment to explain patiently what he meant by the phrase, and then flipped open one of the other magazines and laid it next to Elaine's. "Both of these photos are of paintings done by the same artist. Can you tell me what you see?"

Elaine studied both pictures quietly. "Well, I see what you mean about the color choices. They are very similar." She grimaced. "But that's what I don't understand. Don't painters use a variety of colors, depending on what they are painting?"

Archie shook his head. "Don't think of it as only using a certain number of colors. Think of it more as a palette. Some artists only work in earth tones. Others favor pastels."

Elaine turned her attention back to the two pictures. "This artist liked jewel tones."

Archie smiled widely. "Exactly. Now you see what I meant when I said I was looking for stylistic similarities. My father would have had those as well."

She nodded. "I understand now. What else should I be looking for?"

"Well…" He paused to scratch his temple. "I understand that brushstrokes can be indicative of an artist, or that some choose to feature a particular detail over and over in their work."

"What kind of detail?"

"Landscapes, for example. Some artists only paint landscapes. Or old buildings."

"Or people?"

"That's right."

Elaine bit her lip, thinking. "Archie, what kind of details do you think your father favored?"

Archie lowered his gaze, but not before Elaine caught a glimpse of heartache in his eyes.

His fingers smoothed his hair so that it lay perfectly against his forehead—a nervous habit he seemed to have picked up in recent weeks. "That is difficult to say. I...did not even know my father was a painter, so to try and pinpoint what styles he favored would be pure speculation."

He fell silent and Elaine could only guess the number of thoughts that were tumbling around inside his head.

"It really does feel as though I barely knew him," he said at last. "It was a bit of a shock to find that as kind and loving a father as he was, he had a side—an entire history—that he kept only to himself."

"Maybe it was too painful for him to talk about," Elaine offered gently.

Archie closed the magazines. "Yes, you may be right. Still, I wish..." He blinked several times and then glanced apologetically at Elaine. "Well, enough of that. I should be getting back to work." He rose and smoothed the wrinkles from his sweater.

Elaine motioned toward the kitchen. "But you haven't had lunch."

He offered a stiff smile. "I may eat something later. You go ahead. I'll take care of any customers who come in."

Elaine gathered the rest of the magazines spread out on the table and placed them into Archie's waiting arms. When she finished, she stepped back and pressed her hands to her hips.

"We can look through them some more after the tearoom closes if you'd like."

Archie looked hesitant. "Actually, I'm expecting a phone call. The company Nathan told me about? The one he thought might be able to authenticate my father's painting?"

Elaine nodded. "Yes?"

"A woman there is supposed to call me this evening to go over the procedure for submitting a work for authentication." He cleared his throat nervously and shifted the magazines to one arm. "Would you and Jan mind...that is, if I were to ask..."

Elaine laid her hand over his arm. "Of course you can take time off to take the painting, Archie. Whatever you need."

He smiled. "Thank you, Elaine."

"Of course." Elaine smiled back. "What does Gloria think about all of this?"

He hesitated. "She was quite intrigued by the whole thing, actually, especially when I told her there was a possibility that I might have to go to New York. She's always wanted to visit that city." Pink colored his cheeks and he lowered his gaze. "She was hoping we might make it a vacation."

"And?"

He looked up. "And what?"

"Are you going to make it into a vacation?" she asked patiently.

"Well, I..." He sputtered to a halt. "I hadn't really considered it. I mean, what about the tearoom?"

Elaine smiled. "The tearoom will be just fine." She gave his hand a pat. "Go on, Archie, and take your wife to New

York. Enjoy your time there, and send back lots of pictures. Okay?"

For a moment, Archie simply stared back at her, wide-eyed, and then his smile grew to match hers. "I think I'll do that, Elaine. Indeed, I shall. Thank you so much. I can hardly wait to tell Gloria. She'll be so excited."

He gave her a pert nod before hurrying off. Elaine sighed with satisfaction. That was one thing that had gone well today. She couldn't be more pleased.

CHAPTER THIRTEEN

Elaine helped Jan close up the tearoom and then went upstairs to change before her Wednesday night Bible study. She and a few of the women from church had recently formed an informal group and had taken to meeting in one another's homes. This week, it was Pearl Trexler who would be playing hostess.

Elaine donned a pair of navy-blue slacks and paired them with a pale-gray sweater and her favorite silver earrings. Finished dressing, she grabbed her purse and slung it over her shoulder, then made her way downstairs. Jan was busy in the kitchen. Elaine followed the clamor of pots and pans and stuck her head inside for a peek.

"Sure you don't want to come with me?"

Jan looked up from a pot of steaming water. She clutched a handful of noodles that she held suspended over the pot while Elaine crossed to join her at the stove.

"And miss my Wednesday night Alfredo?" She dumped the noodles into the pot and gave them a stir. "I think not."

Elaine took a deep whiff of the sauce simmering on the back burner. "*Mmm.* I'm almost tempted to join you." She took a step back and eyed Jan carefully. "Except I wouldn't want to intrude on you and Bob."

"No worry there," Jan said without looking at her. "He's not coming over. Said he had to pack."

She gave the spoon a tap against the side of the pot and then set it on a curved cast-iron holder Elaine had picked up at a garage sale.

Worry pricked her heart. Jan hadn't said much since telling her of Bob's plans, but Elaine sensed the multitude of things she'd left unspoken. She set down her purse. "I could stay if you like. I was teasing earlier, but I really don't need to go if you'd rather not be alone."

Gratitude shone in Jan's eyes as she met Elaine's gaze. "You don't have to do that."

"I wouldn't mind," Elaine insisted. "You know how much I enjoy your cooking."

Jan shook her head stubbornly. "I thought you said you were meeting Nathan afterward for a late supper?"

"I was, but I'm sure he would understand if I had to change our plans."

"You don't have to." Jan grabbed Elaine's shoulders and gave her gentle push toward the door. "Go on, and have fun. Tell the ladies hello for me."

Though she sounded adamant, Elaine still hesitated near the door, wishing she knew exactly the right words to say and terrified she'd pick the wrong ones. Finally, she licked her lips nervously and clutched the strap of her purse.

"Jan?"

"Yes?" Jan looked up curiously.

"I just wanted to say that I love you, and I'm praying for you. And Bob. For both of you."

Elaine stumbled a bit over the words, but the gratitude that rose in Jan's eyes told her it didn't matter. Sometimes, people just needed to know that someone cared.

"Thank you for the prayers, Elaine. I love you too."

Elaine nodded. "You're welcome."

Hitching her purse strap higher on her shoulder, she reached for the door to the garage and let herself out. Elaine shivered as she opened her car door. Fall had certainly decided to creep up on them early this year, and she doubted it would be long before the leaves changed color or the first flurries flew. Not that she minded. Elaine always enjoyed the changing of the seasons, and autumn with all its wonderful scents and sights was her favorite.

For all of their money, the Trexlers' home was completely cozy and unassuming. Pearl welcomed Elaine from the threshold of their cheery yellow door and led her toward the living room, where a variety of voices already hummed with excited chatter.

"I heard Martha lost her grandmother's diamond earrings," Kit Edmonds was saying to the other nine or ten women gathered. "Poor thing. I heard she was devastated when she learned they were gone. Something like that just cannot be replaced."

Elaine sat in one of the empty chairs that had been brought out from the kitchen and set next to the fireplace. She leaned toward Rue Maxwell, who was hanging on every word Kit spoke with rapt attention. "Martha lost her grandmother's earrings?"

Rue glanced at her. "Oh, hi, Elaine. Sorry, I didn't see you come in. Yes, Martha and George Wittmer are the latest in the string of robberies to hit Lancaster. You haven't heard?"

Elaine's breath caught in her throat. Martha and George had just returned home after traveling to Vermont to attend his mother's funeral. And now this?

She shook her head. "No, I didn't know. When did it happen?"

Rue's eyes widened. "Last night, I think."

Elaine sighed sadly. What was happening to their little town? "Was anything else stolen?"

"Not that I heard. Kit went by there to visit with them today and she was just filling us in on everything Martha told her." She lowered her voice and leaned in close. "Martha asked us to pray for George. He's taking this pretty hard, what with his mother's passing and all."

"Of course." Elaine took a pen from her purse and scribbled George and Martha's name on an old bulletin stuffed inside her Bible so she wouldn't forget to add them to her prayer list later. Her pen poised over the paper, she glanced at Rue. "Um, you wouldn't happen to know the Wittmers' address, would you?"

"Not off the top of my head. Kit would know."

Elaine clicked the top of her pen and returned it to her purse. She'd have to wait until she could talk to Kit to see if her hunch about the addresses played out. "Is there anything else we can do for the Wittmers?"

Rue nodded. "Pray their dog is found. Martha told Kit her little wiener dog got out while the intruder was in the house. They haven't seen him since."

"How did he get out?"

"Apparently the intruder got in through the sliding glass door off their kitchen. Martha found it still partly open."

"Oh no. Poor Martha. I know she loves that little dog. Has she tried calling the animal shelters nearby?"

"According to Kit, she has. The dog has a chip though, so if he is brought in, they ought to be able to get him back to his family."

"Well, that's good." Elaine shook her head and made a mental note to add the lost dog to her prayers for Martha and George.

It took several minutes for the excited chatter to die down, as everyone had some new tidbit to share about the break-ins plaguing their community. Finally, Pearl lifted her hand and called everyone's attention to their reason for coming.

"I'm sure we are all quite concerned about the things that have been happening around Lancaster," she began. "Maybe it would be a good idea for all of us to take a little extra care about locking our doors and windows at night, at least until this person is caught."

Several heads nodded in agreement.

Pearl took out a pencil and held it above the notepad on her lap. "Now aside from Martha and George, is there anyone else we should be adding to our prayer list?"

They went around the room, with several people adding names of church members who were ill, or family members with prayer concerns. Elaine added Priscilla, and then silently added Jan while Pearl prayed. Though she knew Jan wouldn't mind being prayed for, she wasn't sure she was ready to have others know about the situation with Bob and so kept the prayer request to herself.

As always, Pearl was well prepared as she led the women in a study of Esther. She handed out several pages of notes she'd found interesting while she researched, and even included a list of reference material for anyone who wanted to delve deeper once their study concluded. Elaine tucked hers inside her purse to examine more closely later, and then followed Pearl into the kitchen after they'd finished the study to help with the refreshments.

Pearl set a pitcher of freshly squeezed lemonade on a tray and then handed a platter with homemade cookies to Elaine.

"Thank you so much for your help," she said, "but you really didn't need to. Don't you get enough of this at the tearoom?"

Elaine laughed lightly. "Apparently not. Besides, I don't mind a bit. I really appreciate you hosting the Bible study tonight."

"Thank you, dear," Pearl said, grabbing the pitcher and carrying it with her back toward the living room. "But it really is nothing. Will and I love having people from the church over, especially for things like this."

Maureen Oakley jumped up from her chair when she saw Pearl and Elaine coming and hurried over to the coffee table to push aside the notepads and materials that were left to make room for the tray.

"Here you go, Elaine. Set that down here."

"Thank you, Maureen." Elaine relieved herself of her burden and then went back into the kitchen to get the napkins and cups she'd seen waiting on the counter. Maureen followed after her.

"Let me help you with something," she said. She grabbed a tall stack of cups and then held them balanced against her arm. "So? How's Jan doing?"

Elaine dropped her gaze to the napkins and took her time arranging them in a pretty fan. "She's doing all right. I'm assuming you've heard about Bob?"

She nodded. "My niece works at the realty office where Bob went to list his house. She overheard him say he'll be leaving for Baltimore next week. Is that true?"

"Unfortunately," Elaine said. She swiveled to rest her hip against the counter.

"Well, I do hope everything works out for her and Bob. They make such a nice couple."

Elaine smiled politely. They did make a nice couple. She couldn't imagine how sad their parting will be. Unless…

An idea sparked in Elaine's head. Maybe they could plan a going-away party for Bob—a way to celebrate his success and Jan's strength in her own conviction. Bob moving was sad, but maybe they could infuse a touch of sweetness into the circumstances. She tucked the idea away to discuss with Jan later.

Elaine gathered the napkins. "Let's get back. I'm sure everyone is waiting."

"Of course." Maureen offered a cheery smile and scurried away as fast as the brace on her leg would allow. For a seventy-year-old woman who had survived polio as a child, she sure could move, Elaine thought, hurrying to catch up. At least she knew Maureen would keep her word about not repeating anything she heard where Jan and Bob were concerned. Maureen had a kind heart, and she truly did care about the other members of her church. Her worry for Jan was genuine, of that Elaine was certain.

Because she had plans with Nathan for dinner, Elaine did not stay to mingle as she normally did. Instead, she wished everyone a good night before heading off toward The Odyssey, where she and Nathan planned to meet. Indeed, he was already seated at one of the rustic tables but rose when she entered, and a tall glass of iced tea awaited her when she sat down.

She took a grateful sip. "Oh, thank you for ordering this, Nathan. I'm so thirsty."

He resumed his seat with a smile. "No problem. How did the Bible study go?" Grabbing hold of his napkin by one corner, Nathan gave it a snap and then laid it over his lap.

"It was very nice. Pearl does such a wonderful job getting the lesson ready. I really think she missed her calling. She should have been a teacher. You should have seen all the notes she prepared for us."

Nathan chuckled in agreement and offered Elaine a basket filled with fresh rolls. Elaine took one and tore off a small piece, releasing a cloud of warm, yeasty scent that made her mouth water. He took one for himself and set it on his plate.

"This place looks busy tonight," Elaine said.

"Sure does. I guess now that the Hearthside is closed, business here will be picking up, especially on the weekends."

"I hope so. I'd love to see this place do well."

"Me too."

She savored the warm bread as she perused the menu. The Odyssey was a small restaurant, but the food was delicious. She especially enjoyed their ginger salmon, which was served under a tangy glaze made of honey and Dijon mustard and topped with slivers of fresh ginger. She laid the menu aside.

"I honestly don't know why I bother looking at that thing. I already know what I'm having."

"The ginger salmon?" Nathan laughed and set his menu atop hers. "Actually, I think I'll join you this time. It looked really good the last time you ordered it."

Elaine swallowed another sip of her tea. "You won't be sorry. The sauce they put on the top is to die for, and the carrot soufflé…"

She broke off as she caught sight of a familiar face seated just a few tables over. Instinctively, Elaine hunched her shoulders, ducking down to hide behind Nathan's broad back.

Nathan eyed her curiously. "Elaine? What are you doing?"

She set down her roll to point discreetly over his shoulder. "Nathan, is that Pasha sitting over there by the window?"

"Who?"

"Pasha. The guy who was with Bedrich Jagr. You remember, he was staying at Lake Country Cottages on the other side of the lake."

"The European guy who nearly killed you? Yes, I remember him." He eased sideways a bit on his seat and cast a surreptitious glance over his shoulder. "Sure looks like him."

The door marking the hallway toward the restrooms opened and Elaine sucked in a breath as Bedrich stepped out.

"*Ooh*, and there is Mr. Jagr himself."

Nathan picked up his menu and pretended to study it. Instead, he studied her over the top of it. "So? The man has to eat, right?"

"Of course," she admitted reluctantly, still watching as Bedrich wove his way through the tables toward the window. "But what do you suppose he's still doing here? I mean, I know he said he was on vacation, but we're heading into the off season now. A lot of places will be closed. Why do you think he picked this time of year to visit Lancaster?"

Nathan picked up a pad of butter and used his knife to spread half of it over his roll. "I think you just said it—it's the off season. He's a lot less likely to run into a bunch of crowds, which is kind of what he wanted, right? At least, that's how he made it sound."

"I suppose," Elaine said, but then hunched lower in her chair when Pasha's head lifted and he appeared to scan the room.

Just then, their waitress appeared, unwittingly blocking Elaine's view of Bedrich and Pasha while she took their orders. Impatient to see what Bedrich was up to, Elaine gave her order quickly and then pointed to Nathan.

"And he'll have the same."

"Good choice," the waitress said with a cheerful smile. "So that's two of the ginger salmon. And would either of you care for an appetizer?"

Nathan raised one finger but Elaine cut him off before he could speak.

"No, thank you. That will be all."

"I'll have it right out." Giving her notepad one last jot with her pen, the waitress walked away quickly to turn in their order.

Nathan eyed Elaine with a frown. "Elaine…"

"What?" she replied, innocently. "You said you wanted the salmon."

"That's true but…"

Once again, Elaine cut him off. She grabbed Nathan's arm, her fingers trembling and her palms damp.

"Nathan."

"Yes?"

Her heart rate picked up speed as a tall form rose to block part of the window. "Um, don't look now but…"

"What is it?" Nathan twisted to look in the direction she was staring, but Elaine held fast to his arm.

"It's Bedrich," she whispered, her eyes rounding as she stared over Nathan's shoulder and then at him. "He's on his way over. And he doesn't look happy."

CHAPTER FOURTEEN

The house was quiet without Elaine there to disrupt the silence with her cheerful chatter. Though it had taken some getting used to, Jan found she loved always having someone to talk to and bounce ideas off of. She sighed as she turned the heat down on the Alfredo sauce and then went to the refrigerator to scout out a jar of Parmesan.

Finding it near the back of the refrigerator, Jan pulled it out and gave it a shake. It felt suspiciously light. Dismay washed over her as she realized she'd forgotten to add it to her grocery list the last time she'd cooked pasta.

She unscrewed the cap. As she'd suspected, only a tiny bit remained in the bottom, not nearly enough to finish her Alfredo sauce. Maybe she could run across the street to Murphy's.

She grimaced as she threw a quick glance at the pasta. She couldn't leave it sitting in the hot water or she'd have a thick, soggy mess when she got back.

Using a tip she'd learned from a cooking show long ago, Jan drained the pasta, then tossed it in olive oil to keep it from sticking. When she got back, she'd boil fresh water and add the pasta for a couple of seconds just to heat it through.

Satisfied with her plan, Jan grabbed her coat and headed out the door. Murphy's General Store carried a limited selection of groceries, but it was only two blocks away and handy to have around when Jan didn't care to run all the way to Waterville for the occasional odds and ends. Mostly, Des Murphy catered to the locals, but the "summer" residents appreciated being able to pop in to nab ingredients for s'mores or a tank of gas.

Bethany Elderberry, the store manager, greeted Jan with a chipper smile as she walked in. "Evening, Jan."

"Evening, Bethany." Jan looked around the nearly empty store. "Slow night?"

Bethany closed the door on the cooler she had been stocking and nodded. "Sure is. I don't love nights like this. Makes the time drag."

Jan looked at her watch. "Well, it's only thirty minutes until closing now. I'm glad I caught you. I'm out of Parmesan."

Bethany pointed to her right. "Aisle three. Or if you want some fresh stuff, I think I got a specialty order in for one of the summer residents who never picked it up. Look in the dairy case."

"Thanks," Jan said. "I'll take a look."

Fresh Parmesan did sound good, and Jan was in the mood to treat herself a bit. She chuckled as she passed up the bottles of dry Parmesan. To think, treating herself nowadays had been reduced to splurging on fresh cheese she would have to grate by hand.

The dairy case was located at the back of the store near a tall bank of windows. Jan quickly found the specialty item

Bethany had told her about and opened the door to fetch it. It wasn't until she closed the door that her attention was snagged by a reflection on the glass.

Henry Philpott?

Jan spun to look. The aisle behind her was empty. She turned back to the dairy case. She was certain she'd seen something on the glass. She grabbed the door and swung it open slowly.

There!

Once again, Jan spied the image of the portly man she remembered from the tearoom. Only the glass wasn't reflecting something in the store, she realized quickly. It was outside and at the house next door.

Rushing to the counter, Jan slapped down two five-dollar bills. "Here you go, Bethany."

"Did you find everything you need?"

Jan held up the cheese. "Yep."

"Wait, don't you want your change?" Bethany called as Jan hurried toward the door.

"No, thank you. You keep it." Jan opened the door and stepped outside.

Henry Philpott was indeed perched on the steps outside the house next door. From the lights fixed on either side of the entrance, Jan could see that he carried a bulky-looking briefcase and had several cardboard tubes clutched under his arm. He lifted his free hand and knocked.

The cardboard tubes could be the maps Rue said he often carried around, but the bag? Jan imagined all sorts of tools and gadgets whose purpose ranged from unlocking bank vaults to picking locks. She knew she was getting ahead of herself, to say the least.

She took her time strolling to her car. She didn't want to draw his attention by appearing too interested, but when she hit the unlock button on her key fob, he jerked and his head swung in her direction.

Sensing she'd been caught, Jan opted to play it cool. She lifted her hand and waved. Instead of waving back, he half-turned his back to her and hurried down the steps to a rather nondescript car with a broken taillight. Jan noticed it the moment he started the engine and drove away.

Now, that was odd. What was Philpott doing out so late, and why had he rushed off the moment he realized she'd been watching? With no answer to either of those questions, Jan knew her only option was to wait for Elaine to get home so she could tell her what she'd seen.

Jan opened the driver's door and set the cheese onto the passenger seat. Things around Lancaster had certainly grown strange in the last few days.

Back home, Jan finished her supper, though it proved mostly tasteless since she couldn't stop thinking about Henry Philpott. When she finished, Jan carried her plate to the kitchen sink and gave it a rinse before adding it to the dish-washer, thankful for the slight nudge in her chest that meant she had someone to wait up for, to watch for, to worry for.

Though she hadn't heard her phone ring, she couldn't help but check the display. No missed calls.

Sighing, Jan slipped the phone into her pocket, turned out the kitchen lights, and headed upstairs. Obeying the demand of her aching feet, she slipped out of her shoes and into a comfortable pair of slippers before sitting down in front of the TV for a quiet night of *Jeopardy*. She normally enjoyed answering the questions along with the contestants, but tonight her mind was too preoccupied by other things to really focus.

"Enough of that." Jan reached for the remote and clicked off the TV. If she couldn't focus on the show, maybe she'd pass the time trying to figure out a different sort of puzzle.

Pushing up from her chair, Jan wracked her brain for the last place she'd seen the newspaper with the picture of the gun used in the home invasions. She snapped her fingers. Under the cash register. That's where Archie had stored it last time. Maybe he'd put it there again.

She headed down the stairs. Sure enough, after rummaging a bit, Jan found the newspaper, which was considerably more crumpled than the last time she'd seen it. Folding it in half, she carried it back up the stairs to the sitting room. Jan flicked on the floor lamp to reread the article. No new information jumped out at her, but this time she was careful to note the date the robberies began. Though it seemed much longer, the first one had occurred just over a week earlier.

She lowered the paper, thinking. The paper said five homes had been broken into, with only minor things missing from a couple of the homes, and nothing taken from others. If only she could figure out what the person was after!

Jan lifted her glasses to rub her eyes. There wasn't much sense pondering that question. She wasn't a mind reader, after all.

A headline at the bottom of the page announcing the closing of one of Lancaster's oldest drugstores caught Jan's eye. She read the opening paragraph and then flipped to the inside to read the rest of the story. Sad. That drugstore had been owned by the same family for over fifty years, but now that the youngest son had passed away from cancer, the family had decided to close their doors.

She moved on to another article about a martial arts club in Waterville that would be competing in a World Championship Meet in Bangor. Martial arts. Jan shook her head. All of that karate stuff was really rising in popularity with the young folks, her granddaughter included. She made a mental note to ask Brian about Kelly's next meet. She didn't want to miss an opportunity to cheer on her granddaughter.

Her gaze slid down the page to a smaller article she'd missed before. The photo that went with the article showed several people attempting poses and one person standing in front of them with his hands raised high, as though directing.

"Community Opera House begins rehearsals," Jan read out loud. She adjusted her glasses and continued reading.

A well-known local actor will be stepping behind the curtain to direct a controversial play this fall. Last month, Maxwell Fisher, known for his roles in such off-Broadway productions as *Shear Madness* and *The Harvest,* announced that he would be directing *Red Princess,* a production about Galya Brezhnev, Leonid Brezhnev's granddaughter. When asked why he had decided to tackle the project, Fisher replied: "I think it is important to keep history alive. This play tells a lot about Russia's history from the perspective of someone who lived it, and from a very unique point of view."

Casting calls were announced earlier this month, and rehearsals began in Waterville this week.

Jan's gaze returned to the photo. So Maxwell Fisher was directing. He was certainly a handsome enough man and one well suited to the theater. Jan had met him briefly, when he had come into the tearoom after it first opened, but she had seen him in various productions over the years. It was fun being acquainted with a person who was something of a local celebrity. She wondered if he had recruited any other locals.

Her gaze traveled over the other actors. Several of them were only pictured in profile, so she did not hold out much hope of recognizing any of them, but one face looked familiar. She squinted for a better look.

The picture was tiny, and the person's face much too small for her to make out any features. Frustrated, Jan set down the paper and got up to dig through her nightstand for a magnifying lens. She found one and carried it back to the sitting room.

Pushing her glasses up onto her head, Jan held the lens over the newspaper photo and studied the faces anew. She was right in thinking one woman looked familiar.

Jan sat back in her chair, astounded. The woman starring in the play was the same woman she and Elaine had seen in the tearoom.

It was Irina.

CHAPTER FIFTEEN

Elaine tensed as Bedrich approached, his brows lowered in a scowl. The man at his elbow wore a matching scowl as he reached out to grasp Bedrich's arm.

"Please, sir. Allow me."

Bedrich gave a curt nod. Pasha stepped forward and Nathan rose to meet him.

He stuck out his hand, stopping Pasha in his tracks before he could reach the table and Elaine. "Hello, gentlemen. How can we help you?"

Pasha lifted his nose, ignoring Nathan's outstretched hand. "You are following us. Why?"

"Following you?" Nathan shook his head and braced both hands on his hips. "I'm afraid there's been some mistake. Elaine and I are out on a date."

"We had no idea you were here," Elaine added, though deep down, she found the experience a happy coincidence. For all his bluster, surely Pasha wouldn't dare attempt anything in such a public place, and possibly she could get more information on the mysterious Mr. Jagr. She sidled up to stand next to Nathan. "But I'm a little surprised that you would think we were following you. Why would we do that?"

She injected a note of innocence into her question as she eyed Bedrich with her eyebrows raised.

"Mr. Jagr is accustomed to drawing attention...," Pasha began.

"But I had hoped to avoid that here," Bedrich interrupted. "Which is why I was so concerned when I heard that you were taking pictures of me without my permission. You *were* taking pictures, were you not?"

His gaze pinned her like a bug to a board. Elaine swallowed nervously. "You certainly drew my interest."

"And why is that?" he asked, almost jovially. He folded his arms across his chest, both Pasha and Nathan virtually forgotten as he stared at her, brown eyes piercing.

Elaine felt a bit of vim and vinegar rise up from her middle. "A foreign diplomat traveling to Lancaster to visit our little tearoom is a rarity," she said. "Anyone in my situation would of course be curious. I'm sorry if my interest threatened you."

Bedrich gave a nod to Pasha, who went back to their table reluctantly. When he had gone, Bedrich's gaze returned to Elaine. "Perhaps you do not understand. It is not your interest that threatens me." He motioned toward one of the empty chairs at Nathan and Elaine's table. "May I?"

Nathan threw a quick glance at Elaine. She nodded. Whatever Bedrich had to say, she wanted to hear it. Nathan reached for his chair, but before he could sit, Bedrich held up his hand. "I wonder if you would allow me a minute alone to speak with your date? There is something of a rather delicate nature that

I would like to discuss with her. I will not keep her from you long, as I am quite certain the two of you are looking forward to an enjoyable evening."

Nathan gripped the back of his chair, his doubt reflected clearly on his face. "I don't think that's such a good idea."

"No, it's all right," Elaine said quickly. She directed a reassuring glance his way. "We won't be long. Please, Nathan."

After much hesitation, he gave a slow nod. Jerking his thumb over his shoulder, he said, "I'll be right over there."

Watching.

Though he didn't voice it, his meaning was clear. Bedrich gave a slight nod to show he understood and then turned his attention to Elaine as Nathan moved away.

"Well, Mrs. Cook, I must say you are something of a mystery."

He circled around to hold Elaine's chair for her. Having him so near raised the hairs on her neck, but she took the seat he offered and then watched as he claimed one of the empty chairs for himself.

"A mystery? Whatever do you mean, Mr. Jagr?"

He put his hand to his chest. "Bedrich, please."

She inclined her head slightly. "And you may call me Elaine."

"Thank you." He gestured to Nathan's untouched glass of water. "If I may?"

"Go ahead."

"Thank you."

He brought the glass to his lips and took a slow sip. Elaine wasn't fooled. He was drawing out this encounter, perhaps hoping to lull her into a false sense of security. But what did he want?

Bedrich toyed with one of the napkins on the table, his long fingers oddly graceful as he coiled the ribbon that bound it around his thumb. "Social media is an interesting beast, yes?" he said at last. "With just a few strokes on the keyboard, a person can post anything, to anyone, anywhere in the world. The Facebook especially has proven to be both a blessing and a curse. Do you agree?"

She blinked, struggling to process this strange turn in the conversation. "That's not what I expected you to say."

"Oh?" He eyed her with interest. He rested both hands atop the table, his fingers clasped.

"Mr. Jagr—"

"Bedrich," he corrected amiably.

"Yes. Bedrich. What is it you are afraid I will do?"

"Why were you taking my picture?" he countered, his voice dropping to almost a growl.

"It wasn't your picture I was taking."

"You…you mean Pasha?" His eyebrows rose and he stopped to glance at the man over his shoulder. He looked genuinely confused as he turned his gaze back to her. "I do not understand."

Elaine feigned coy shyness. "It's silly, really. Do you remember an actor by the name of David McCallum? He played a Russian spy named Illya Kuryakin in a 1960s TV series called *The Man from U.N.C.L.E.*"

Now it was Bedrich's turn to appear confused. His eyes narrowed. "I do not recall a program by that name. Regardless, I am not sure I understand what this has to do with my friend."

She covered her mouth as though she were attempting to stop a giggle from escaping. "Pasha looks like him."

Which he did. But that was secondary to the fact that he also carried a gun exactly like the one she and Jan had found in the tearoom—a fact she had no intention of revealing.

Bedrich did not appear convinced. He studied her in a calculating sort of way that raised gooseflesh along her arms. Tilting his head to one side, he chuckled ruefully, though his gaze hardened. "So you are determined to keep your reasons private. So be it. I cannot force you to explain what you were doing or why." He pushed away from the table, started to rise, and stopped. "I will however, ask that you respect my privacy...and I will do my best to respect yours."

"Excuse me?" Though the words were not of themselves in any way threatening, there was no mistaking his tone. Elaine tensed as he settled back into his chair.

Bedrich motioned to her with his index finger. "Your husband. He was a military man, was he not? From all accounts, a fine, upstanding soldier—one dedicated to his family and his country."

Elaine waited, sensing there was more he had yet to say.

"He was highly decorated. I'm sure he must have made you proud. Was it difficult, traveling all over the world?"

"How do you...?" Suddenly, she remembered. She'd told him at the cottages. She clamped her lips shut.

"I know a great deal about your family, Elaine." Bedrich leaned forward to brace his elbows on the table, and his voice dropped so he was heard by her alone. "I know about your husband. It would be a shame, would it not, to see the reputation of such a respected man tarnished? One false word, spoken indiscreetly, could cause irreparable damage to a man unable to defend himself. Or the family he left behind."

Comprehension dawned. Bedrich's eyes glowed as he watched her face, and a satisfied smile appeared on his lips.

"I see we understand each other."

He reached out to pat her hand. Elaine jerked away before he could. Bedrich shook his head.

"Forgive me. I do not relish the use of such tactics, but surely you can see that just as you desire to protect your husband's memory, so I must take steps to protect myself and my family."

He pressed his large hand to his chest, and a bit of the harshness left his gaze. "I am not a popular figure, here or abroad. In my country, there are many who would gladly risk their lives in an attempt to take mine. You are correct in assuming I am not here simply for enjoyment, but what business I do have, I am not at liberty to discuss. I hope you will not endanger my life with your careless curiosity, because I will protect myself, Elaine, by whatever means necessary." He rose abruptly and gave a slight bow. "And now, good evening."

Air came and went from Elaine's lungs in shaking, halting breaths. Bedrich wove slowly back to his table, as though he hadn't just uttered a thinly veiled threat, as though he made them every day. In moments, Nathan hurried to her side, as edgy and panicked as Bedrich had been calm.

"That didn't look pleasant. Are you all right? What did he say?"

Elaine motioned for him to wait, watching as Bedrich and Pasha picked up their coats and moved toward the exit.

Nathan's chair scraped the floor and then he sat heavily. "Elaine? What did he say?"

Elaine reached for her purse with trembling fingers. "Nathan, would you mind if we got our food to go? I'm not hungry anymore, and I really would like to get home."

Anger darkened his face. "Why? What did Jagr say? Did he threaten you? Where did he go?"

His head swiveled back and forth as he searched the restaurant. Elaine grabbed his hand and squeezed.

"Nathan, please. I appreciate your defense of me, but I really would like to go, if you don't mind."

His gaze fell to her their clasped hands and then he cupped hers in both of his. "All right. C'mon. I'll get your coat." He motioned to the waitress and quietly explained that they would be taking their meal to go before settling their bill. When he finished, he returned to the table. His face no longer looked flushed, but worry shone in his eyes and Elaine regretted having been the one to put it there.

Nathan moved to pull out her chair. "Ready?"

She stood and gave him smile. "I'm ready. Thank you, Nathan." And then, to show that she really did feel better, she put her hand on his arm. "Why don't we go on back to the house? We can eat our dinner in the kitchen. I'll make us a pot of tea afterward and we can sneak some cookies out of the freezer to go with it. As long as you don't tell Jan."

At her teasing, a look of relief washed over him. He pushed his hands into the pockets of his trousers and nodded. "Sounds good. Let's go."

In the parking lot, Nathan made certain Elaine was tucked safely into her car before walking off toward where his car was parked a few spaces down. He was such a dear, and so attentive. His protectiveness made her feel cherished, wanted...loved.

Elaine watched him climb into his car. Only when she pulled on to the road did she let her defenses fall enough for tears to wet her eyelashes. Bedrich's demeanor had taken her completely off guard, but the threats he'd made against Ben?

Suddenly, the seat belt felt too tight. Elaine shifted on the seat and checked her mirror. Nathan's headlights covered her in a reassuring glow. He would expect an explanation when they reached the house, and Elaine couldn't blame him, but for reasons she couldn't explain, she found herself reluctant to tell him what Bedrich had said. But how long could she hold him off? What would she say?

CHAPTER SIXTEEN

The patter of footsteps assailed Elaine the moment she and Nathan opened the door. Elaine barely had a chance to shrug out of her coat before the kitchen light flipped on and Jan poked her head into the hall.

"Elaine! There you are. I've been waiting for you..." A flush colored Jan's face pink as she slid to a stop upon catching sight of Nathan. "Oh, hi, Nathan."

"Hi, Jan."

Jan pointed to the bag stamped with The Odyssey logo in his hand. "What's that?"

Elaine crossed to a peg next to the door to hang her coat. "Our dinner. I'll explain later." She shot a glance at the clock on the wall. "I thought you were planning to go to bed early."

The sparkle of excitement returned to Jan's eyes. "You'll never believe who I saw tonight."

Elaine glanced around the kitchen. "Saw here?"

Jan gave a flick of her wrist. "Not here, at Murphy's. We were out of Parmesan so I ran over to get some, and guess who I saw through the window at the house next door? Henry Philpott," she continued, before Elaine could guess.

Nathan followed as they walked to the kitchen, and set the bag of food on the counter. "Who is Henry Philpott?"

Briefly, Elaine explained and then turned back to Jan. "What was he doing there, Jan? Could you tell?"

"Unfortunately, no." She made a carrying motion with her hand. "He had some kind of bag with him, though, and several long cardboard tubes like you'd use to store posters."

"His maps?" Elaine asked.

"That was my guess too. I tried to get close enough to see what he was up to, but he didn't wait around long enough for me to figure it out. The moment he spotted me, he scatted off of those steps like a spooked cat and drove away."

"Hmm."

"But that's not the most interesting thing." Jan beckoned with one hand. "Come see what else I found."

She whirled and led them to the table, where a newspaper lay spread across it. Next to it laid Jan's magnifying lens, a pencil, and small package of Post-it notes.

Elaine eyed the items critically. She picked up the Post-its and wagged them. "What in the world have you been doing? What is all of this?"

Jan scooped up the paper and waved it toward Elaine. "Do you remember the article we saw the day we found the gun in the tearoom?"

"Of course," Elaine said with a puzzled frown. How could she forget? The article was what had sparked her suspicion that the person responsible for the home break-ins had been in the tearoom. She circled around to the other side of the table where she and Nathan both sat. "What about it?"

"Well, while you were gone, I decided to take another look at that story." She glanced at Nathan. "Sorry, you probably have no idea what we're talking about."

He shook his head. "It's all right. Archie told me."

"Good." She turned back to Elaine. "Anyway, I didn't find anything new in the story about the break-ins."

"Okaaay." Elaine frowned. So far, she had no idea what could possibly be causing the excited gleam in Jan's eyes. "So what did you find?"

"Look."

Jan turned the paper toward her and jabbed her finger on to a small feature article near the bottom of the page. Both Elaine and Nathan leaned in to see.

"It's the picture," Jan said. "Who do you see?"

"I don't…" Elaine spread her hands in exasperation.

"Is that Maxwell Fisher?" Nathan asked.

Elaine nodded. "It looks like him, but…"

"Yes, it's him. But look at the woman." Jan handed Nathan the magnifying lens. "Use this. I needed it to be sure, but I'm almost certain it's…"

"Irina!" Elaine grabbed the lens from Nathan and held it over the woman's face. "Look, Nathan. This is the woman I told you about, the one with the European-sounding accent. Only she doesn't really have one."

Nathan's gaze bounced back and forth between Jan and Elaine, both of who were staring at him earnestly. "Hold on. What doesn't she have?"

"An accent," Elaine said, "only I forgot to tell you—well, actually we didn't have time because we bumped into Bedrich—but her accent was fake all along."

Jan grabbed her arm. "You bumped into Bedrich? When?"

"Tonight, at dinner. That's why we decided to bring our food home."

Nathan held up his hand. "All right, this is getting confusing. Can we tackle one thing at a time?"

Elaine let out a rueful laugh. "You're right." She looked back at Jan. "Tell us about Irina."

Jan gave an eager nod and slid into the chair across from Elaine's. "All right. So, apparently, she's the lead in a play that Maxwell Fisher is directing called *Red Princess*."

"I've never heard of it," Nathan said.

Jan tapped the newspaper. "Me either, but the article says it's some kind of controversial play about Galya Brezhnev, Leonid Brezhnev's granddaughter."

Nathan lifted his hand to his chin. "Which could explain the accent, right?"

"Maybe," Elaine agreed, "or maybe it could provide good cover."

"For what?"

She shrugged. "That's the part we haven't figured out yet." She turned to Jan. "What else?"

"Well, the article says that Irina and several other members of the cast are friends of Maxwell's—people he met when he was performing in New York. They agreed to be in his play as a favor to him, or something like that. The article wasn't exactly clear."

"Interesting."

"I thought so too." Once again, Jan picked up the magnifying lens and held it over the photo. "And look, there's Matthew too. At least, I think it's him. It's hard to tell because he's in profile."

Elaine squinted, but hard as she tried, the photo's fuzzy quality in the newspaper made his features difficult to discern. "I don't know, Jan. It sort of looks like him, but we'd probably have to check with whoever took the photo to be certain."

All three of them bent to see whose name was in the photo credit, but it wasn't someone any of them recognized.

"You could ask Candace, couldn't you?" Nathan asked. "She could probably introduce you to whoever took the picture."

"Or we could pay a visit to Maxwell Fisher," Jan suggested.

"Do you think he would talk to us? We only met him that one time he came to the tearoom," Elaine said. "I doubt he even remembers us."

Jan shrugged. "I'm sure we can think of something."

"Of course." Elaine pushed up from her chair. "I'll put on some coffee."

"At this hour?" Jan pointed to the clock above the sink. "Elaine, it's after nine."

"Yeah, and I should really be going." Nathan rose with Elaine and went to stand beside her. "I have a big auction this weekend that I need to get ready for."

Elaine's gaze drifted to the bag from the restaurant, still sitting on the counter. "But we haven't eaten our dinner!"

His lips turned up in a crooked smile. "That's okay. This late at night, it would probably give me heartburn."

He placed a quick kiss on her forehead and then motioned toward the door. "I'll let myself out."

"Nathan, wait." Elaine glanced at Jan. "I'll be right back."

Though she looked curious, Jan merely nodded and watched as Elaine followed Nathan out to his car.

When they reached the driver's door, Elaine fidgeted with her collar uncomfortably, waiting for the question she knew Nathan had yet to ask, but still uncertain how she would answer it.

Finally, she lowered her gaze to the pavement under her feet, afraid to meet his eyes. "So, um, we didn't really get a chance to talk."

"No, we didn't."

He said nothing more, and only the sound of the night wind stirring the trees filled the sudden silence. Was that all he had to say? Elaine summoned the courage to look up at him.

"Aren't you . . . that is, didn't you want to know . . . ?"

Nathan watched her fumble a moment, then stepped toward her to grasp her arms gently. "Elaine, when you're ready to tell me, you will."

Inside, a part of her argued that she should explain, that he deserved to know what Bedrich had said, and yet an equally obstinate part urged her to wait, to sort out her feelings, to think about Ben.

She startled as she realized that the thing keeping her from opening up to Nathan was her memories of Ben—and worry that if she told Nathan of her concern, she would be hurting him unnecessarily. And why? Hadn't it taken her months to sort through all of those old feelings? Hadn't she scrutinized them and prayed over them and given all of the old hurt of losing him over to God when Nathan came along? Without a doubt, she loved Nathan and believed he loved her, but would she be breaking his heart if she told him that there was a part of her that also still loved Ben, and always would?

"Hey." Nathan touched her chin lightly, encouraging her to lift her eyes to him. "Are you okay?"

"I'm fine," she whispered. "I'm sorry, Nathan. We'll talk soon. Okay?"

He gave a small smile, but she saw the twinge of hurt that flickered in his eyes. "Okay."

He lifted her hand and pressed another brief kiss to the back before reaching for the door handle.

"Nathan?"

He paused to look at her. "Yeah?"

"I really am sorry." The wind kicked up and a lock of her hair swirled into her eyes. She brushed it aside impatiently. "It's ridiculous, I know, but I need time to sort a few things out."

He nodded, and then it was his hand that brushed her hair aside. His fingers ran slowly down the length of it, lingering when he reached the end, and tugging ever so slightly. "I trust you, Elaine. I promise I'll be patient."

For a long moment, he looked at her, and then the door opened and the dome light flashed on, washing his face in its pale-yellow glow. "I'll call you tomorrow."

"All right." She retreated a step and watched as the tail-lights on his car blinked out of sight. Deep inside her heart, an old ache flared to life.

"Oh, Ben."

She whispered his name on a sigh, surprised that it was him she called out to and not Nathan. Not the Lord.

Pressing her hand to her chest, she turned and went back inside where Jan waited. She was seated at the table, still perusing the newspaper, but she looked up when Elaine entered, and her lips turned in a worried frown.

"What was that all about?"

What could she say? She didn't know herself. She moved to the cupboard and took out a cup. "I'm going to make myself some tea. Would you like some?"

"Tea? I thought you wanted coffee."

"I changed my mind. I'll have enough trouble sleeping tonight as it is."

"*Hmm.*" Jan rose to fetch the kettle. "I'll help."

The faucet turned on, the hollow sound of the water filling the kettle the only noise in the now quiet kitchen. Elaine selected a couple of tea bags and placed them into waiting cups while they waited for the water to boil.

"I have some maple croissants left over from this morning. Would you like one?"

Elaine shook her head, and then changed her mind when she heard her stomach growl. "On second thought, I am pretty hungry."

Jan smiled knowingly and plucked two from the plastic container where she kept the extras and set them on a plate. Elaine followed her to the table.

"Listen, before we talk about me and Nathan, would you mind if I ran something by you?"

"Of course." Jan placed one of the croissants in front of her and then motioned for her to continue.

Elaine took a deep breath and dove in. "What would you think about throwing a going-away party for Bob?"

Jan's eyes widened. "What?"

"Sorry. I know that wasn't what you expected." Elaine explained the reasoning behind the going-away party. "It would be a wonderful way to say bon voyage. Maybe we can even sing 'Jolly Good Fellow,'" she said with a chuckle. Then she sobered, crumbling a piece of the croissant between her fingers nervously. "What do you think?"

Jan paused for a moment, then let out a long breath. "I think it's a wonderful idea."

"Really?"

She nodded. "It'll be good for everyone to see that I'm all right and that I'm fully behind Bob's decision. Besides, it'll be fun. I'll get to work planning out the details." She got up and fetched two napkins while Elaine took a nibble from one of the croissants. "Now that's settled, so tell me what happened at dinner."

Elaine chewed slowly, swallowed, and finally looked into her cousin's eyes. "Bedrich Jagr was there with that hulk of a bodyguard, Pasha."

Jan froze, then slowly laid one of the napkins near Elaine. "And?"

"He was quite angry when he saw me and Nathan there."

She pulled out a chair and sat. "Why? It's a public restaurant."

"Yes, but he accused us of following him."

"Well, you weren't. You and Nathan had dinner plans. Did you tell him that?"

"Of course, but I don't think he believed me. And listen to this—he insisted that I call him Bedrich."

Jan drew back. "That's rather familiar, isn't it? Did he say why?"

"An attempt at being friendly?"

"Right." Jan's look said she didn't buy that for a moment. The kettle whistled and she rose to get it.

Elaine took another small bite of her croissant. "Anyway, he asked to speak to me alone."

Jan frowned as she poured the water into the cups. "Nathan was okay with that?"

"Not really, but I convinced him to do it so I could hear what Bedrich had to say."

Jan's expression said she wasn't happy as she replaced the kettle on the stove. "Okay. So what did he want?"

"At first, I wasn't sure, but he made his intention clear pretty quickly."

Jan's eyes rounded as she carried the cups with her back to the table. "That doesn't sound good."

Elaine pushed the plate of croissants away. The same part of her that had resisted telling Nathan what Bedrich had said now squirmed uncomfortably.

Jan set down the cups and grabbed Elaine's hand. "He didn't threaten you, did he?"

"Sort of. Well, not me directly." She swallowed hard and pulled her hand away to wrap her fingers around the cup. "He threatened Ben."

Jan blinked in confusion. "I don't understand."

Drawing a deep breath, Elaine stumbled through everything Bedrich had said and implied. Too anxious to sit any longer, she rose to pace.

"He knew Ben was in the military, Jan, and all about his commendations. He knew we'd been all over the world, though, to be honest, I probably supplied that information when I told him that Ben and I had traveled extensively." Elaine shook her head in disbelief. "But what about the other stuff? How could he possibly have learned so much in such a short amount of time?"

"Apparently he has some pretty powerful connections."

Elaine shuddered as all the plotlines from every *Mission: Impossible* movie she'd ever seen replayed in her head. "Well, it was certainly enough to impress me. Bedrich had me so shaken up, Nathan and I left the restaurant right after that."

"Oh dear. I'm sorry." Jan fingered the handle of her cup, her tea as yet untouched. "It does make one wonder, however, why he felt compelled to confront you. Did he give you a reason?"

"You mean besides trying to scare me out of snooping?" Elaine asked. "And by the way, it just about worked. I've never been so frightened." She grimaced. "Or possibly it was because he really is afraid I will inadvertently sabotage whatever secret mission he's on. But if that is the case, why did he bother talking to me at all?"

Jan chose that moment to take a sip from her cup. At Elaine's words, she nearly choked on her tea. "Secret mission. Are you serious?"

"I am, actually." Elaine passed her a napkin and then explained what Bedrich had said about not being at liberty to discuss his purpose in Lancaster.

"That really does sound mysterious," Jan said, dabbing the tea from her mouth. "But without any way of knowing more, trying to figure out what he's doing here is just about useless."

"We could do what he accused me of and follow him around town," Elaine suggested. "Maybe we'll get lucky and see who he's meeting with."

Jan shook her head adamantly. "After he threatened you? I don't think that would be wise."

Elaine had to agree. Besides, risking her reputation was one thing, but Ben's? She reached for the croissant on her plate but didn't bother taking a bite. It would likely be tasteless. Instead, she merely toyed with the food until it lay in crumbled bits on her plate.

Jan watched, her eyes narrowed and her lips pursed thoughtfully. "What did Nathan have to say about all of this?"

And there it was. Her very insightful cousin didn't miss much.

Elaine picked up a piece of the croissant and rolled it between her fingers. "The truth is, I didn't exactly…"

"You didn't tell him?"

She looked up, her face warming guiltily. "Not yet. I mean, he asked, but I wasn't sure I wanted him to know."

Jan's eyes widened incredulously. "Why not? You've never wanted to keep anything from him before."

What could she say? Her husband's face flashed before her eyes, and pain pricked her heart in a way that it had not in many months. She dropped the croissant and brushed the crumbs from her fingers.

"I am falling in love with Nathan, Jan. But as much as I care for him, I'm still protective of Ben."

"Of course you are," Jan said. "That's completely natural and understandable."

Elaine looked a little unsure, but continued on. "And today, when Bedrich made those threats, my first instinct was to fight for him. And Nathan is a remarkable man, and I just don't want him to worry about me." She shrugged as Jan nodded. Elaine felt her eyes well with tears. "Anyway, it's so ridiculous. Anyone who knew Ben would know his character was above reproach."

"Absolutely."

"And yet something about Bedrich's manner filled me with fear. If he's powerful enough to dig into my past with Ben, what would stop him from planting something incriminating?"

"Possibly nothing," Jan said quietly. "I think you should tell Nathan, Elaine."

She agreed, of course. Elaine nodded slowly. "I know, and I will eventually. After I've had time to think all of this through."

Jan drew a deep breath and stretched her arms over her head. "Yes, well, try not to do that tonight. It's late, and we have a long day ahead tomorrow."

Elaine glanced at the clock. "Huh?"

"It will be Thursday. Rose has a test, remember? We're going to be shorthanded."

She groaned. "I forgot all about that."

Jan hid a yawn behind her hand as Elaine stood to carry their cups to the sink. "I didn't. Thank goodness we have Archie. We'll need him for sure tomorrow."

Elaine placed the cups carefully in the sink and then ran a bit of warm water over them. "Speaking of Archie, has he mentioned anything to you about authenticating his father's painting?" She turned from the sink, careful to keep her features neutral and composed.

"He's found someone?"

Elaine nodded. "In fact, it's a connection that Nathan recommended. The only hitch is that the authenticator works out of New York. Archie would have to take the painting there. Gloria has always wanted to see New York, so I suggested that he take time off and make it into a little vacation."

Jan gave a wave. "Oh, no problem. That's a good idea. I hope he gets all of that resolved soon. The poor dear has seemed so distracted lately." Jan yawned again and rubbed wearily at her eyes. "Well, I'm off to bed. Good night, Elaine."

"Good night, Jan," Elaine said, her thoughts already winging back to Nathan. She would need to talk with him. Soon. But first she intended to grab a bite to eat and try to figure out what Bedrich was really doing in Lancaster.

CHAPTER SEVENTEEN

J an rose early the next morning—earlier than usual—and did as much of the baking as she could so that she would be free to help out in the parlors if she was needed. Thankfully, she only had to step outside of her kitchen twice, once just before lunch, and again just before they closed. The second time, it was to wait on Priscilla, so Jan didn't mind so much. She was glad to see that Priscilla seemed to have gotten over the break-in to her home. She smiled often as she chatted with Jan, and her cheeks bore a rosy glow that Jan found very becoming.

She set a second pot of hot water on the table for Priscilla, who thanked her as she refilled her cup.

"Not working at the library tonight?" Jan asked.

Priscilla shook her head and reached for a packet of sweetener. "Not tonight. It's my day off."

"Ah, well then, are you sure I can't get you something to go with that tea? Our cookie of the day is a white chocolate and macadamia."

Priscilla's cheeks turned pink. "No, thank you. They sound delicious, but I actually have plans for dinner. I'm meeting

Curtis Hanson. He offered to help me look for a new door. Something that offers a little more security than the one I have now."

"Oh. That was nice of him."

Priscilla agreed with a smile. "He really is a very kind man. Very thoughtful."

"That's wonderful. I'm glad he's helping you," Jan said, then smiled as she went back to the kitchen. She placed a stack of dirty dishes in the dishwasher and punched the start button. It was good to see neighbors pitching in to help their neighbors. With everything going on in recent days, it sort of renewed her faith in people.

Jan had just finished cleaning the kitchen when Bob appeared at the back door, a lopsided smile on his face and a bouquet of flowers in his hand.

Jan's heart rate sped up as she waved him in.

"Hi," he said carefully, holding out the flowers. "I hope you don't mind my dropping in without calling first."

Jan accepted the flowers shyly. "Don't be silly. You don't have to call. There's something I wanted to talk to you about anyway."

"Really?"

"Uh-huh." She crossed to the cupboard, removed a glass vase, and carried it to the sink to fill it with water. Bob followed her there, his hands shoved deep into his pockets and a look of chagrin on his face that made him appear boyish and charming.

"So . . . this feels a little awkward."

Jan stopped fidgeting with the flowers to look at him. "I know. I'm sorry about that."

"Me too." He cleared his throat. "You wanted to talk to me about something?"

"Yes." Though she didn't want to, she forced herself to ask the question simmering on her tongue. "How's the packing coming?"

"Okay. I've got just about everything ready to go, and I'll have the rest shipped later, after the house rents."

"Sounds like a good plan."

"Thanks."

"But before you do that, Elaine and I were wondering how you would feel about us throwing you a going-away party?" Jan rushed on nervously. "It would be Sunday. You wouldn't have to do a thing. We'll take care of all of the details. And we could have it here so you wouldn't have a mess to clean up afterward."

To her relief, Bob looked almost pleased by the idea. "That would be nice."

"Good. So it's settled. I'll call you with the details."

Bob pulled his hands out of his pockets and motioned toward the door. "Listen, Jan, I was hoping maybe we could have dinner together. That is, if you're free."

"I'm free," she said, almost too quickly. Then, so as not to sound too eager, she added, "I'll have to freshen up first."

"Not a problem. I'll wait however long it takes."

Jan pondered his words as she scurried up the steps. He'd meant he'd wait while she changed for dinner, but what if it *had* been more? Would she want him waiting for her indefinitely?

Yes!

The answer came almost immediately. Oh, but this was hard. Much harder than she'd expected.

After slipping into a comfortable but stylish blue blouse and a simple pair of khakis, Jan went back downstairs. Archie had long since gone, but Elaine was there chatting with Bob. Both looked up as she entered.

"Well, I'll let you two get going." Elaine moved toward the doorway, sending Jan an encouraging thumbs-up as she passed. "Have fun," she whispered before she disappeared down the hall.

Jan turned to Bob.

"Ready?" he asked.

At her nod, he turned and went into the hall to fetch her coat from the hall tree. He held it while she slipped her arms in, and then his hands lingered lightly on her shoulders while she fastened the buttons.

"Okay, all set."

His smile as he held the door for her set her heart to fluttering. After so many years of being alone, it was astonishing how quickly she had grown accustomed to all the little nuances that went with being a couple. She relished them all—the hand at her back as she exited the car, the door held for her as they walked into one of their favorite restaurants, the chair pulled out for her as she sat.

"I hope The Garden is okay," Bob said. He grinned and picked up the basket of bread and offered her a slice. "I had called ahead and reserved us a table, just in case."

"Of course it is. I love this place." Jan thanked him for the bread and set it on her plate, then leaned forward to rest her elbows on the table. "You do realize where we're sitting?"

Bob looked around bemused. Though several customers packed the small Italian restaurant, this alcove was secluded and protected from most of the bustle.

Recognition dawned and another grin curved his lips. "Is this the same table where we sat the first time we came?"

Jan nodded, happy that he'd remembered. "The restaurant was busy that night. I recall thinking how lucky we were to get such a nice table away from all of the clamor."

"Looks like this is our spot," he said with a wink. Slowly, the mirth faded from his face. "Sorry."

She forced a cheery note into her voice. "Why? It's not like you're falling off the earth for goodness' sake." She grabbed a bottle of oil and herbs, gave it a swirl, and then poured a small amount onto her bread plate. "We'll still be friends. And I promise that the next time you're in Lancaster, it'll be my turn to treat."

Instead of laughing with her, Bob's face became solemn. He picked up his butter knife and tapped the end against the table. "Tell you what. Let's make an official date. Say around the end of October?" His gaze sharpened earnestly. "Planes fly both ways, Jan. I could come back to Lancaster for occasional visits, and you could come to Baltimore. In between, we'll Skype, or FaceTime, or whatever the kids do nowadays. What do you say?"

Before she could say anything, their waitress appeared. Jan scrambled to pick something from the menu and then stared at Bob while he chose a simple lasagna and dinner salad.

When the waitress left, Bob folded his hands atop the table and leaned toward her. "So? What do you think?"

"I'm not sure," Jan admitted. Laughter erupted nearby, and she waited until the noise died down to continue. "Long-distance relationships are never easy, especially when there isn't a specific time frame to work toward."

He reached out to claim her hand. Bob was a lawyer. His hands would never have the same callused feel that Peter's had, but his grip was warm and tender, and the slight tremble she felt spoke of the depth of his feelings.

"People do it all the time, Jan. We won't even have to be home to take a call like in the old days. We can talk on our cell phones or computers any time we want."

"Yes, but it's still not the same as being together face to face."

"I agree, but that's what the trips to and from Lancaster will be for. We're not a couple of broke teenagers. We can afford to fly a couple of times every other month. More if we want."

He was fighting for her, for their relationship. She should have been thrilled.

Struggling against the longing of her heart, Jan slipped her hand free. "Bob, please trust me when I say that more than anything, I would like to believe that a long-distance relationship could work for us."

"It can. I know it can."

"To what end?"

His brows knitted as he looked at her. "What do you mean?"

"I mean, we date for a few months and then what? Do you intend to move back to Lancaster?"

His lips pressed into a thin line.

"I'm sorry, Bob."

"Me too."

Jan fidgeted uncomfortably. "Do you want to leave?"

He looked up and even managed a weak smile. "Why? We're still friends, right? And friends can have one last dinner together."

Friends? She gulped back rising emotion at the suddenly insipid word. The last thing she wanted was to merely be his friend. But neither did she want to give up the opportunity to share these last few, precious moments.

She picked up her water glass. "To friends."

"Friends." Bob touched his glass to hers and then took a sip. Jan did the same. "So the eggplant Parmesan, huh? I didn't know you liked eggplant."

Heavens, was that what she'd ordered?

"I thought I'd try something different."

Bob laughed, completely unfooled by her poor attempt at covering her mistake. "If you don't like it, I'll let you have half of my lasagna."

Jan laughed. "Deal."

Now that the difficult things had been said and some of the awkwardness had passed, Jan found herself relaxing and enjoying their time together. Bob studiously avoided any further mention of Baltimore, and Jan pretended not to notice as she filled him in on everything that had been happening at the tearoom the last few days while they enjoyed their meal.

Afterward, Bob paid their bill and then excused himself to wash his hands. While she waited for him to return, Jan people-watched. She was glad to see so many come and go. It meant The Garden was enjoying a good amount of business, which in turn meant she could enjoy the eggplant parmesan again, which had turned out to be not so bad.

Her nose tickled, and Jan reached into her purse for a tissue. She looked up just in time to see a man enter.

Matthew?

She adjusted her glasses for a better look. Sure enough, it was Matthew, but this time, Irina wasn't with him. He waited at the cash register while one of the waitresses put together his to-go order, which gave Jan ample opportunity to study him discreetly.

He stood with his back to her for some time, yet it was easy to see that he was dressed in some kind of uniform. He wore dark slacks and a heavy coat with a wide faux-fur collar. On the arm was a shield or badge of some sort, and underneath the coat, a light-blue shirt was visible. He looked like a police officer. How could that be?

Jan started to stand up for a better look. As she did, Matthew turned sideways. He definitely wore a utility belt under his coat. She caught a glimpse of a nightstick at his hip as he took his to-go order.

"Jan?" Bob watched her, a puzzled smile on his face. "What are you doing?"

"I was just…" She turned back to the cash register in time to see Matthew exit with his food. She slapped her hand against her thigh. "I saw Matthew."

"Matthew. The guy from the tearoom?"

She nodded and pointed toward the cash register. "He just left."

"Was Irina with him?"

"No, but I think he was wearing a uniform."

"He's in the military?"

"Not that kind of uniform. Like a police officer or a security guard." She paused, her thoughts whirling. "Bob, I need to know where Matthew was going. If we hurry, I think we can follow him."

Bob's eyes widened. "Follow him? But that's..." He blinked as she reached for her purse. "You're serious."

"Yes." She rose and stood looking at him. "Well? Are you coming?"

He gave an incredulous shake of his head as he reached for his coat. "I have to admit, I'm going to miss these adventures, Jan. Let's go."

Out in the parking lot, Jan spotted Matthew climbing into a dark sedan. On the door was some kind of magnet sign, but the car was too far away for her to read what it said. She pointed.

"There he is."

Bob nodded and hurried with her across the parking lot to his car. Inside, they buckled up and watched as Matthew pulled on to the road.

"There's not a lot of traffic tonight," Bob said. "It should be easy to see where he's headed, but I won't be able to follow too close or he'll spot us."

Jan agreed and clutched the dashboard tightly as Bob turned onto the road behind Matthew. After making several slow sweeps through two different neighborhoods, Jan began to fidget.

"I don't understand what he's doing. Where is he going?"

"It really is strange," Bob said. "It's almost like he's just meandering through these neighborhoods."

Jan's muscles clenched. "Or maybe he's casing them."

"What?"

"Maybe he's looking for houses without lights or cars in the driveways. It's possible, right?"

Just then, the car Matthew was driving made a sudden right turn. Though he'd been some distance behind, Bob was forced to swing around the block. By the time they circled back, Matthew was gone.

Jan blew out a frustrated sigh. "Well, so much for that. I think I'm ready to head home, if you don't mind. Elaine needs to hear this."

He nodded. "You got it."

CHAPTER EIGHTEEN

Elaine stared at Ben's picture. Time had dimmed the sharp pain she felt when she looked at it, and tears no longer burned her eyes when she took in the lines and details of his face. But every now and then...

She sighed, letting her fingers linger on the glass before she replaced the photo on the mantel above the fireplace in the east parlor. She loved this picture of Ben. The ribbons on his chest never failed to fill her with pride, a sentiment she knew he shared every time he put on his dress uniform. She couldn't bear to think of his memory unfairly tarnished.

Maybe Jan was right. Maybe she should ask Nathan for his opinion. Except that when she did, she'd also have to admit to him that though she had come to love him, a part of her heart still belonged to Ben and always would. And she didn't want to hurt Nathan, not for anything in the world.

There was still over an hour before the tearoom opened. Typically, Fridays were not their busiest days, but Elaine had heard Jan walk down to the kitchen early that morning. She poked her head through the doorway and saw Jan punching a lump of dough. On her face was a look of deep concentration, and small wisps of hair clung to her forehead.

Elaine moved to the coffeepot. "What did that dough ever do to you?" she joked.

"I'm making fresh bread," Jan replied, no trace of humor in her voice. She delivered another solid punch to the dough and then draped a cloth over the bowl.

Elaine took a mug from the cupboard. "Want some coffee?"

"No, thanks. I've already had tea."

"Really? What time did you get up?"

Jan ran her thumb under her eyes, inadvertently calling Elaine's attention to the fact that they looked quite red—whether from crying or lack of sleep, she couldn't be certain. Maybe both.

Elaine poured her coffee, then brought the cup to her lips but didn't drink. Instead, she studied Jan over the rim. "Want to tell me how…?"

"I saw Matthew last night," Jan interrupted. "I would have told you last night but you'd already gone to bed and I didn't want to wake you." She carried the bowl over to the counter next to the stove. "I'll just let that rise here."

Caught off guard, Elaine lowered the cup. "You did?"

"Uh-huh. He was at the restaurant. I saw him waiting for a to-go order." Jan moved to the sink and squirted some soap into her hands.

"Really?"

"Yep. And it looked like he was wearing some kind of uniform."

"Any idea what kind?"

Jan bumped the handle on the faucet with her elbow and water poured into the sink. "A security guard maybe? Or a police officer. It had some kind of emblem on the shoulder similar to what they wear, but that's not the most interesting part. When he left the restaurant, he ended up driving through several neighborhoods."

"You followed him?"

Finished washing her hands, Jan grabbed a towel and rubbed them dry, then flung the towel over her shoulder and crossed to the table.

Elaine pulled out a chair and joined her there. "Okay, so tell me. What exactly happened?"

Briefly, Jan filled her in. "He wasn't driving a police car, so he couldn't have been on patrol, right?"

"Maybe he's a detective?" Elaine offered, and then sized up the uncertainty on her cousin's face with a glance. "But you don't think so?"

"I'm not sure. That could explain why he had a gun, I guess, but why didn't he come back to the tearoom to get it? And why would he have been driving a plain car, but wearing a uniform?"

"I guess I don't know," Elaine agreed.

"Right. And it was an Italian gun, remember? I suppose it's possible, but would someone working for the United States be carrying something like that?"

She had a point. Stumped, Elaine picked up her cup and took a sip.

"Besides," Jan continued, "the way he drove through those neighborhoods looked suspicious to me. I got the feeling he was looking for something."

Elaine frowned. "Except, if your first guess was right, and he does work for a security company, he could just have been making rounds."

"True," Jan said. She blew out a sigh. "Well, it should be easy enough to find out where Matthew works. I could call around to the local police departments and security companies."

Elaine took another drink from her cup and then rose from the table. "Well, I suppose I had better get upstairs and get dressed."

"Wait, Elaine. Don't you want breakfast? I could fry up a couple of eggs if you like."

Elaine laid her hand over her stomach. "No, thank you. My tummy is a little upset. I think I may have caught some kind of bug."

Actually, she was pretty certain it was worry about what Bedrich had said about Ben that had her stomach in knots, but she didn't say so to Jan. She hurried upstairs to dress and by the time she went back down, Rose was busily preparing the tearoom for opening. Elaine grabbed an apron and went to help.

"Good morning, Rose. How did you do on your test?"

Rose beamed as she looked up.

"She passed, just like I knew she would," Jan said. She carried a tray of freshly washed cups into the parlor and set them on the table.

Rose smiled. "Thanks, Jan. I only missed one question. They asked what I would call a leavening agent made from a dry acid or acid salt, baking soda, and starch or flour."

Jan's brow furrowed as she thought and then quickly cleared. "Baking powder?"

Rose nodded, her admiration for Jan evident in her smile. "Very good, Jan. I drew a blank when I read the question during the test, and then I ran out of time before I could go back to it."

Jan patted her shoulder gently. "Still, you did very well to only miss one question. I'm sure your professors are proud."

She hunched her shoulders humbly. "I hope so. Now that we have all the basic terminology down, we'll start testing our skills and knowledge in the kitchen next semester." She rubbed her hands on her pants nervously. "I'm so glad you're letting me help with the baking. I'll need to be ready."

"Don't be silly," Jan said fondly. "I'm glad to do it."

Elaine turned away to stack the cups Jan had washed in the china hutch. Of course her thoughtful cousin wanted to help, but she wondered if Jan realized what it would mean when Rose finally finished her classes.

A few minutes later, Archie joined them, but as Elaine had feared, it was hardly worth his time. Business was slow, and she found herself glancing at the clock often. At eleven thirty, she sent him home so he and Gloria could finish packing for their trip to New York, and then she ducked into the office to check her e-mail. Even that seemed slow. Only three new messages, and one was a sales ad. She sighed.

"Are you okay?" Jan asked from behind her.

Elaine looked up, startled. "I didn't even hear you come in."

Jan smiled. "Want to tell me what's on your mind, or can I guess?"

Elaine frowned.

Jan patted her shoulder. "Have you thought about going by the library to see what you can find out about Mr. Jagr? It might help you feel better."

"I suppose." Elaine bit her lip, thinking. "I could go by there after the tearoom closes."

"Why not now?"

"I couldn't do that."

"Why not? We've been slow all morning, and it's time for your lunch anyway."

She had a point, but still Elaine hesitated.

"Go on," Jan urged. "Rose and I can handle the tearoom."

Elaine fidgeted with the phone while she debated. "I suppose I *could* make a quick trip."

"Oh, go on," Jan said with a knowing smile. "I'm just as curious as you are. And anyway, we might just as well get something done, and with business this slow, it won't be anything here."

Elaine replaced the phone, her mind made up. "Okay, but I won't be long."

Jan's wave said she wasn't worried, so Elaine snatched up her purse and coat and hurried out the door.

While business at the tearoom had been slow, business at the library was not. Several patrons crowded around a long table, and several more waited at the counter while Priscilla checked them out.

Elaine wandered over toward the nonfiction shelves. There were several interesting books, but none that looked current enough to answer her questions about Bedrich. Nearby, a row of computers caught her eye. The screen on one of them still glowed brightly from the last user.

Elaine left the book aisle and slid into the chair. She wiggled the mouse until the cursor jumped to life, and then typed "Bedrich Jagr" into the search bar. Several links appeared, but none that matched his name completely. She narrowed the search by adding the words "Czech diplomat" and waited while the rainbow wheel spun.

Still nothing, but the word "Czech" did snag several news sites, all of which seemed to be talking about a missing collection of rare stamps.

Elaine scrolled past them impatiently. Could it be that Bedrich had a different name? Perhaps Bedrich was his middle name, or even a nickname. She searched Jagr with the word diplomat, but that only brought up a hockey player.

Frustrated, Elaine stared quietly at the screen, her index finger tap-tapping the mouse.

"Elaine, is that you? I thought I saw you come in." Priscilla ducked into her view, smiling.

Elaine leaned away from the computer screen. "Oh, hi, Priscilla. Yes, I'm on my lunch break. Sorry I didn't say hello. You looked pretty busy. Is there some special library event going on that I don't know about?"

Priscilla laughed. "It's book clubs mostly. There are a couple of groups around town who meet here once a month." Priscilla motioned toward the screen. "What are you looking for?"

Elaine pouted and crossed her arms over her chest. "Would you believe a list of Czech diplomats?"

Priscilla's lifted in surprise. "What?"

Elaine gave a wave of her hand. "Never mind." She turned the screen so Priscilla could see the links leading to articles on the missing stamps. "Have you heard about this?"

Priscilla eyed the computer, then pulled out a chair and sat next to Elaine. She fell silent as she skimmed the headlines, and then she sat back with a nod. "Oh yes. That robbery was quite a big deal a few weeks ago. You didn't know about it?"

Elaine shook her head. "I guess not. What happened?"

"Apparently, a collection of rare Czech stamps was stolen from a house in"—she paused and turned her gaze to the screen—"Prague, I think it was, or somewhere near there."

"Any idea who took them?"

"Not yet. The culprit is still on the loose."

Elaine laid her finger against her lips. "But why stamps? If you're going to break into someone's home, why not take something more valuable?"

Priscilla's eyes widened and she laid her hand over Elaine's arm. "Are you serious? Surely you realize some stamp collections can run into the millions of dollars."

Elaine turned her gaze back to the computer. "Really? I mean, I knew some stamps were valuable, but I had no idea there were stamps worth that much."

Priscilla reached over to the keyboard and searched for rare stamps. Instantly, several links popped up, and even more images of individual stamps whose value climbed into the hundreds of thousands.

"That is unbelievable," Elaine said, her mouth dropping open as she spied a Benjamin Franklin stamp worth $935,000.00.

"I told you," Priscilla said, laughing. "Of course, not every stamp is worth that much, and not every collection is either."

"But the one stolen from Prague is, according to that last article."

Priscilla nodded and pushed the keyboard back toward Elaine. "Anyway, were you here looking for something in particular, or were you just interested in diplomats? And stamps."

Elaine jerked her head up to stare at the clock on the wall. She had already been gone twenty minutes longer than she'd wanted to be. She frowned. "Oh dear. I've lost track of the time. I should be getting back."

"Priscilla?" The man who had been helping Priscilla choose a home security system ducked into view.

"Oh, hello, Curtis."

He smiled broadly. "I just stopped in to say hello. I hope you don't mind."

"Not at all." Priscilla motioned toward the counter. "Do you know Elaine?"

"We've met."

He greeted Elaine politely and then looked back at Priscilla. Though he claimed he only wanted to say hello, something on his face said he wanted more.

Priscilla seemed oblivious. She motioned toward the far end of the library. "We got more of those World War II magazines you like. You're welcome to take a look."

"Oh, okay. Thanks." Curtis's shoulders dropped slightly as he nodded and walked away.

Elaine rested her elbows on the desktop. "Well, now, what was that all about?"

"Curtis?" Priscilla's brows lifted innocently. "Just a friend. He comes in here quite a bit looking for research material. He's interested in anything having to do with World War II."

"I'd say that's not all he's interested in."

Priscilla snorted. "I hardly think so."

"Why? He can't be too much older than you."

Priscilla fidgeted in her seat. "Actually, he retired early. He's only fifty-six."

Elaine spread her hands wide. "Okay, so then . . . would it be a stretch to imagine yourself on a date with him?"

Priscilla seemed to consider this a long time. When she did speak, her voice held a nostalgic note that Elaine had not expected.

"Did I ever tell you about Charles?"

"Who?"

"The boy I met just after college."

Elaine shook her head and Priscilla went on.

"He was two years older than I was, but so much fun to be around. I met him at a church gathering one of my friends was hosting. He was talking to some guys about a mission trip he was planning that next summer. I remember thinking what a remarkable person he was to have such a promising career ahead but still care about doing the Lord's work."

Her smile seemed distant somehow, as though she were slipping into that place, so many years ago.

"Not long after that, Charles and I started dating." She smiled happily. "Oh, but those were wonderful times. I had just finished earning my master's degree in library science, and he was working as an engineer."

Elaine fell silent, surprised and intrigued by this new revelation. "I never knew this about your past."

Priscilla dropped her gaze. "It's difficult to talk about, I suppose. Though we had our differences, at the time, they hardly seemed to matter. I truly thought he was the man I was going to marry. And Charles felt the same way. In fact, I'm pretty certain he would have proposed had it not been for..."

She broke off and a sigh that spoke of heartache and lost love slipped from her lips.

"What happened, Priscilla?" Elaine asked quietly. "Why didn't he propose?"

Slowly, Priscilla drew her gaze back to Elaine. "September 11 happened. Several of Charles's friends enlisted. Shortly after, he did too. I shouldn't have been surprised. He was a real patriot and he believed in doing what he could for his country."

She drew a long breath, and even before she said the words, Elaine knew.

She squeezed Priscilla's fingers. "Where was he killed?"

"Afghanistan." She met Elaine's gaze squarely. "It's so strange. Sometimes it seems so long ago, and other times, it's like it happened yesterday."

"I know."

Her eyes widened and then quickly filled with tears. "I'm sure you do."

Elaine dropped her hands into her lap. "You never wanted to marry, after Charles, I mean?"

She shook her head. "Oh, I thought about it from time to time. The first few years were hard, mostly because it took me that long to come to grips with the idea that he was really gone. And then…it seemed as though the years had passed me by. I'd missed my chance at wedded bliss, or so I thought." Her smile returned, dispelling some of the sorrow Elaine read in her gaze. "I'm forty-one years old, Elaine. I'm certainly no spring chicken."

"Neither am I," Elaine said, "but love still found me, even when I wasn't looking."

"That's true," Priscilla said thoughtfully.

"All I'm suggesting is that you leave yourself open to the possibility of love. Regardless of the hurt you've faced in the past, finding someone you love and who loves you back is always worth the risk. Just make sure you're honest with them, and with yourself."

Even as the words left her lips, Elaine knew she needed to heed her own advice. She owed it to herself and Nathan, and she owed it to Ben's memory, no matter how many threats Bedrich Jagr dared to make.

A customer rang the bell at the counter, and Priscilla tossed a glance that way and then back at Elaine. "Thank you for listening."

Elaine smiled. "It was my pleasure. Now, I need to get back to the tearoom, and after that"—she smiled and wagged her fingers in good-bye—"I need to talk to Nathan."

CHAPTER NINETEEN

Elaine pondered the missing stamps as she drove back to the tearoom. Surely it was too far-fetched to believe that Bedrich had a link to the stamps. The simple fact that they were both Czech was not reason enough to suspect a connection. Or was it? Added to that was Bedrich's appearance in Lancaster on a "secret" mission just days after the stamps were stolen. Could it be? And why would a diplomat—someone well-traveled and who would typically have broadened his palate—have such strange, uninspired taste in tea? Well, the last thought could be personal preference, but he was certainly worth investigating.

She pulled into the driveway and noted the number of cars parked outside, glad to see that business had picked up. Once inside, she peeked into the east parlor and noted that Rose had things well in hand. She signaled her return with a wave and then ducked into the kitchen, where Jan was busy preparing a plate of her famous maple croissants. She wiped a smattering of powdered sugar from her cheek as Elaine entered.

Her eyebrows rose. "You're back already? I thought I told you not to rush."

"I didn't, and I was gone over an hour." Elaine grabbed a fresh apron and tied it snugly around her waist.

"Really?" Jan glanced at the clock. "Huh. So? Did you find out anything?"

She put the plate of croissants on a tray and added a steaming pot of water. A second later, Rose entered and whisked the tray away.

Elaine gave herself a mental shake. "I found out about stamps."

Quickly, she summed up the information she'd found in the articles. When she finished, she crossed her arms, thinking. "It simply can't be a coincidence, can it?"

"What can't?" Rose entered bearing several empty cups and placed them on the counter next to the sink.

Once again, Elaine explained what she'd learned. "And I was just saying to Jan," she continued, "that I didn't think Bedrich's appearance along with the robbery of those stamps could possibly be a coincidence."

"Oh, I don't know. It's not all that strange," Rose protested. "The poor man can't help where he's from, after all. That would be like blaming a robbery in London on Archie simply because he's British."

"I'm afraid I have to agree with Rose," Jan said. "Bedrich Jagr doesn't strike me as particularly pleasant, but that doesn't make him a criminal."

Elaine pondered this a moment and then shook her head. "But think about it. What if the stamps somehow ended up in

Lancaster? That would certainly explain the rash of break-ins we've been experiencing, wouldn't it?"

"How on earth would the stamps end up in Lancaster?" Jan asked. "And in the home of one of our friends to boot?"

"And I thought the homes that were broken into weren't robbed?" Rose added.

"Some of them were, and some of them weren't," Elaine said. "But even when something went missing, it was never anything of great value."

"But it doesn't add up, Elaine. Jagr is a diplomat. Surely that means he has some wealth. What does he need with a set of old stamps? Besides, if he's as powerful as you say, couldn't he hire someone to do his dirty work, assuming he really is after those stamps?"

"Someone like Pasha?"

The three fell silent for a moment, and then Rose turned to study Elaine. "What did Jan mean by 'if he's as powerful as you say'? What don't I know?"

An embarrassed flush washed over Jan's face. "Sorry, Elaine," she whispered.

Elaine dismissed her apology with a shake of her head. "Don't worry. I don't mind."

Turning to Rose, she explained what Bedrich had said and the threats he'd implied against Ben.

"Well, that's just *terrible*," Rose sputtered. "Ben Cook was a wonderful man."

Both Jan and Elaine stared at her in surprise.

"Not that I ever met him personally," Rose continued, crossing her arms. "I'm merely going by what I've heard the two of you say, and I've never known either of you to exaggerate."

Elaine shot a quick smile at Jan. They had developed something of a family at the tearoom. She reached out to pat Rose's arm.

"Thank you, Rose."

Her cheeks flushed red. "Don't mention it. Now, about this Jagr guy. I don't like that he had the nerve to threaten you, but is that enough to cast suspicion on him for anything more than bad manners?"

"Maybe." Jan pulled out a chair at the table and sat. Her gaze drifted to Elaine. "But I'm beginning to think he may be worth investigating."

"Me too," Elaine exclaimed, her excitement building.

"Hold on now." Rose paced to the kitchen sink and back. "Didn't you say Priscilla Gates's home was broken into? What could he have been looking for there?"

"Well, she did travel recently," Elaine said.

Jan nodded. "And so did Bob. He made a trip out to Baltimore. His home was broken into while he was gone, or soon after he got back."

"And George and Martha Wittmer," Elaine whispered. "They went to Vermont for his mother's funeral."

"They all traveled," Jan said, her eyes round behind her glasses.

"And how much do you want to bet they all flew into the same airport?" Elaine asked. "There's one way to find out."

"I'll call Bob."

"And I'll call Priscilla."

Rose's head swiveled as he followed the conversation between Elaine and Jan. "What should I do?"

"Take care of the customers," the cousins replied in unison.

They scattered in opposite directions—Jan to the office, Elaine to fetch her cell phone, and Rose into the parlor. A few minutes later, Elaine reentered the kitchen, her cell phone clutched to her chest. Jan leaned against the counter, waiting.

"Well?" she asked.

"Augusta," Elaine said.

Jan nodded. "Bob too."

"And I bet if we check with Martha, we'll hear the exact same thing."

"Should we call her?" Jan motioned toward Elaine's cell. "Do you have her number?"

"I think so. We exchanged numbers when we started the women's Bible study." Elaine scrolled through her contacts and quickly found Martha. She dialed the number and waited while the phone rang. After two rings, Martha picked up.

"Hello?"

Elaine flashed a thumbs-up to Jan. "Hello, Martha? This is Elaine Cook."

Hoping to find out what she needed to quickly, Elaine explained why she was calling. Unfortunately, Martha was in a particularly chatty mood, and Elaine listened while she bemoaned everything from the weather, to the terrible flight from Vermont, to the loss of her grandmother's earrings.

"I mean, honestly, Elaine, what is this world coming to when a person's home is no longer their haven? It's downright pitiful."

"I agree, Martha," Elaine said quickly, "and speaking of your flight, which airport did you say you and George used?"

"Oh, why, Augusta, of course. It wouldn't have made sense to drive all the way to Bangor."

"No, it wouldn't," Elaine agreed.

"But at least we found Buddy," Martha continued, hardly pausing to draw a breath. "Did I tell you we got him back? Thank goodness for the chip George insisted we get him. He was missing for several days, but a shelter in Waterville called this morning and said someone had brought him in. George picked him up this afternoon, and now he's sleeping safe and sound in his little bed, the poor dear. This has been such a traumatic experience for us all."

"I'm so glad you found him, Martha," Elaine said. Before Martha could continue, she added, "Listen, it's been wonderful chatting with you. I'm awfully sorry about your grandmother's earrings. I hope you get them back too."

"So do I. Not that they were expensive, but they had priceless sentimental value."

"Of course. I'll see you Sunday at church, right?"

"I wouldn't miss it."

After a few more pleasantries, Elaine disconnected and sagged against the counter. Jan watched her, smiling.

"That was a lot of work for one small piece of information," Elaine said.

"But was it worth it?"

She straightened and laid her phone on the counter. "It sure was. Martha and George flew into Augusta, just like Bob and Priscilla."

Jan pinched her bottom lip. "Well now, that is interesting, especially considering the other little tidbit of information we uncovered."

"The addresses?" Elaine pressed her palm to her forehead. "I forgot to ask Martha for hers."

Jan waved her hand. "No need. I have it right here." She rifled through a stack of books next to the phone until she found the church directory. She flipped to the back. "Let's see. Wittmer…Wittmer…here it is." Her eyes widened as she looked up at Elaine. "8114 Ash Lane. We were right, Elaine."

Elaine's heart pounded. "Do you thinks it's enough to report to Dan? I could ask him to stop by."

Jan checked her watch. "I think so, but do you think we could ask him to come around to the back door? With everything that has been happening around town, we wouldn't want to alarm our customers."

"Yes, you're right," Elaine said. "I'll call him right now."

She dialed the number. When he answered, she quickly explained her reason for calling and then spent the next half hour watching the minutes tick by on the clock.

At a quarter after three, his car pulled into their driveway. After promising to fill Rose in on everything the trooper said, Elaine quickly shooed her out of the kitchen, then went to collect Jan. Together, they led Dan into the office.

"Thank you so much for coming, Dan," Elaine said as she partially closed the office door. "I realize this was very short notice."

"Not a problem," he said. "I'm always happy to help." He removed a pair of dark sunglasses and slipped them into his pocket, then looked from Jan to Elaine. "Why don't we start by you two telling me everything you uncovered with your unofficial investigation?"

CHAPTER TWENTY

Jan lifted her eyes to the trooper. "I suppose we should explain."

"That might be good," he said, his lips twitching.

Jan stretched her hand in the direction of the kitchen. "Can I get you something to drink?"

"Water would be nice."

"Of course." Jan took a couple of steps toward the door and stopped. "What about a snack? I have some of my oatmeal raisin cookies left. Would you like one or two?"

"You know I won't turn down anything you've baked," Dan said with a smile.

Jan hurried to fetch the food. When she returned, Dan sat near the desk and Elaine sat next to him. He took a small notepad and a pen from the pocket of his shirt. Flipping open the notepad, he turned to Elaine.

"Now, why don't we start at the beginning? You said you've spoken to several people who have had their homes broken into?"

"Three," Elaine said. "I suppose that counts as several."

Jan set the plate of cookies and a glass of ice water next to Dan, then went around the desk to sit. "All three took trips recently," she said.

"And all of them flew out of the same airport," Elaine added.

"And of course, we already told you about their addresses," Jan said, "but you should know we just checked the church directory for George and Martha Wittmer—and it fits the pattern."

Dan wrote that down. "Can you give me the names of the people you spoke to?"

Elaine nodded and named Bob and Priscilla, pausing to give him time to write. When he finished, she looked to Jan. "I suppose we should tell him what happened with Matthew."

Dan looked from one to the other. "Who?"

Jan explained who he was and everything that happened after they left the restaurant. "He just drove through the neighborhoods in a random pattern," she said. "I would even classify his behavior as strange, except…"

"Except?"

"Well, he was wearing a uniform." She gave him a brief description. "If he was on patrol…"

Dan shook his head. "I don't know of any officers in this area named Matthew. And you'd think I would know. We're Lancaster, not New York City."

They smiled. "There is one more person you should probably check into," Elaine said when Jan finished.

He looked up curiously. "Who is that?"

"A man named Bedrich Jagr."

"He's not from Lancaster," Jan said, "but he may have flown through Augusta around the same time as all the others."

Briefly, Elaine explained who Bedrich was and what he claimed to be doing in Lancaster. "Later on, he admitted he wasn't really vacationing," she said, "but he refused to divulge any more information, other than to imply that it was some kind of secret mission."

"Is there any way you could do a background search?" Jan asked. "Maybe find out what he's really doing here?"

"If he truly is a diplomat," Dan said, "he'll more than likely have some kind of immunity."

"Actually..." Elaine bit her lip.

"Yes?"

"We're not entirely certain he *is* a diplomat. For that matter, we can't say positively that he hasn't committed a crime. Now, he does have a bodyguard with him, which is what interested me in the first place. I mean, you don't see many people wandering around Lancaster with a bodyguard, right? His name is Pasha, and I should tell you, he carries a gun similar to the one we found in the tearoom. "

At this, Dan added a note to his notepad and underlined it. Then, while Jan listened, Elaine described how she had researched his name and stumbled across the story about the stolen stamps. She finished by explaining why she thought the two might be connected. "I know it's not much," she said, "but it might be worth looking into."

He nodded and scribbled something on his notepad. "Possibly. Now, what did you mean when you said you weren't sure he's a diplomat? Is that just because you weren't able to find any information about him online?"

"Oh, that." Elaine gave a sheepish grin. "This is going to sound strange, but it's because he ordered black tea."

"I don't understand. Why is that important?"

Briefly, Elaine told him about Bedrich's visit to the tearoom and then her trip to the cottage where he was staying. "Both times, he drank black tea with lemon, which isn't all that unusual, except that he says he's a diplomat. It's been bothering me, but I just now realized why."

"I'm still not clear on why this is important," Dan said.

Seeing his puzzled frown, Jan said, "Elaine and Ben were stationed in several different countries all over the globe while he was active military. She's always been fascinated with other cultures and their histories, but her travels have allowed her to learn all sorts of interesting facts regarding the origins of various teas."

Elaine nodded. "That's right. And while Bedrich does seem to have some influence, he really doesn't fit the profile of other foreign dignitaries I've met."

Dan leaned forward, his eyes gleaming with interest. "What kind of profile is that?"

Elaine folded her hands in her lap. "Well, for example, I met a few dignitaries abroad while traveling with Ben, and I remember that they had gone through extensive training regarding the culture of the people where they would be serving. They were taught everything from social customs, to dress, to the kinds of food common to that area. Typically, this resulted in wide and varied tastes, something Bedrich does not seem to have acquired. You see, while black tea with lemon may be common in the Czech Republic, it is not elsewhere. It seems to me that a man with experience as diverse as Bedrich claims to have would have expanded his horizons a bit."

While Elaine talked, Jan studied the expressions flitting across the trooper's face. She had always known him to be a kind man but honest in his opinions and well trained as an officer. If the things she and Elaine were telling him were not worth noting, he wouldn't pretend otherwise.

Dan added a few more lines to his notepad before flipping it closed and slipping it back into his pocket with the pen. "This has all been very interesting, ladies. Thank you very much." He directed his gaze toward Elaine. "I'll check into this Bedrich Jagr fellow and see what I can find out."

"Thank you," Elaine said.

"Yes, thank you," Jan echoed. She followed the trooper to the door. "And if there is anything more you need from us in the meantime, please don't hesitate to ask."

"I'll do that."

By now, they had reached the back door. Dan put his hand on the knob, then paused and looked back at Jan. She held her breath while she waited for him to speak.

"Listen, Jan, I, uh, ran into Bob the other day. We were both in court for a case he was trying."

Jan's brows rose. "Oh?"

He tilted his head to scratch his temple. "He told me he'd decided to take a job in Baltimore."

"Yes, that's correct. He leaves next week, in fact. We're throwing him a going-away party on Sunday. I hope you can make it."

"Yeah, that's what he said." Again, he paused, his eyes warm with compassion. "He asked me to keep an eye on you. Said he would appreciate it if I stopped over from time to time, just to see how you're doing."

Jan clasped her hands tightly. "He did?"

He leaned closer and laid his hand on her shoulder. "Anyway, he didn't ask me to tell you that. I just thought you should know."

"I…I appreciate that, Dan. Thank you."

He smiled kindly, then reached for the doorknob and let himself out.

CHAPTER TWENTY-ONE

Elaine didn't mean to eavesdrop, but she couldn't help but overhear when Dan mentioned Bob. Rather than listen in to a conversation she had not been invited to, she slipped out to the parlor to see where she could help Rose. The tearoom wasn't full, but there were a few customers scattered about. Elaine stopped by several tables just to say hello, and to check to see if anyone needed anything. A few tables over, Bristol Payson appeared to be in deep conversation with Anita Picard, one of the town's selectmen. Her hands waved in agitation as she talked.

"So anyway, Anita, I really would just like to know if there is anything you can do about this Philpott guy. At the very least, I thought you and the other selectmen should be aware. Apparently, Mark and I are not the only ones he's talked to."

Elaine angled herself toward the table. "Hello, ladies." She smiled and then looked at Anita. "Good to see you both here."

"Hi, Elaine," Bristol said.

Anita returned her smile. "Hello."

Elaine gestured toward the table, and the half-eaten scone on Anita's plate. "How is everything?"

"Wonderful," Anita said. "I love these new scones. Not too tart, not too sweet. They're just right."

"I'm glad you like them. I'll be sure to tell Jan."

Anita nodded and Elaine looked over at Bristol. "How about you, Bristol? Can I get you anything?"

She tucked a lock of blonde hair behind her ear. Elaine couldn't help but notice that her cheeks were flushed and her eyes were overly bright. Whatever she and Anita had been discussing certainly had her worked up.

"No, thank you. I'm fine."

Elaine nodded and then shrugged a little sheepishly. "Did I hear you say a man named Philpott spoke to you and Mark?"

Bristol looked a bit surprised, but she nodded. "Earlier this week, in fact."

"It wouldn't by chance have been a man named *Henry* Philpott, would it?"

Her mouth dropped open. "He talked to you too?"

"Not exactly," Elaine said, pushing her hands into the pockets of her apron. "He came into the tearoom a few days ago." She frowned apologetically. "Do you mind if I ask what he talked to you about?"

"Mining rights, of all things." Bristol grimaced and gestured toward Anita. "I was just telling Anita here that he was a bit too pushy for my taste. The guy showed up at a quarter after nine at night, for heaven's sake."

"What are mining rights?" Elaine asked, her gaze bouncing from Bristol to Anita.

"Apparently, Mr. Philpott works for a company that is interested in doing some drift mining in this area," Anita replied.

Bristol's head bobbed in agreement. "Philpott's job is to get local residents to sign a release of liability against the company he works for."

"I'm not sure I understand," Elaine said. She clasped the back of the chair. "Why would a mining company need a release of liability?"

"Drift mining can produce *horizontal* stresses on the surrounding rock structure," Anita explained. "Enough pressure can cause failure in the rock beneath outlying land or homes."

"And even if there's no drift mining," Bristol said, her color rising, "just setting off exploratory charges could cause the ground to become unstable. Mark and I weren't comfortable signing the release and told Philpott so."

Elaine lifted her eyebrows. "But he didn't want to take 'no' for an answer?"

Her scowl deepened. "That's putting it mildly. He practically told us we were being foolish and unreasonable, and that our fears were unfounded. He claimed there was no reason we shouldn't sign since most of our neighbors already had."

"Was that true?"

"Depends on your definition of *most,* I suppose. We asked our closest neighbors. Some really did sign, but a few others had concerns, just like Mark and I did. All the people who said no complained of the same thing—that Philpott was rude and pushy. He even came by later in the week and talked to Mark a second time. He's lucky I wasn't home, that's all I can say." Bristol tapped her fingernails against the tabletop angrily. "Fortunately, Mark took care of him."

"What did he tell him?" Elaine asked.

"He told him that he was trespassing and that he would call the police next time he caught him on our land. We haven't seen him around since."

Elaine turned her gaze to Anita. "Has anyone else spoken to you about this?"

"No," Anita said, "but that may just be because they aren't sure who to talk to." She pointed toward Bristol. "Bristol and I are friends, so she knew she could talk to me. Unfortunately, I'm not sure there is anything I, or the council, can do. The man hasn't broken any laws."

"There's a noise ordinance," Bristol said, a trifle facetiously. "Can we cite him on that? The man does talk an awful lot."

Anita laughed. Elaine was just glad to see both women's sense of humor returning. She motioned toward the kitchen.

"Tell you what, I'm going to get you both a couple of those scones to take home with you. Maybe that will help brighten your day."

"It'll brighten mine, for sure," Anita said, pushing her plate toward Bristol. "You have to try this."

Bristol pinched off a bite and popped it into her mouth. Slowly, a look of pleasure crept over her face. "*Mmm.* That really is delicious." She looked at Elaine. "I'd love a couple, but you don't have to give them to me. I'll be glad to pay for them."

"Nonsense. I'll be right back."

Elaine hurried back to the kitchen to inform Jan of what she'd learned. While Jan packed the scones into two small boxes, Elaine spilled all Bristol had told her about Philpott.

"That *is* interesting."

Elaine grabbed the boxes of scones and headed toward the door. "I'll be right back," she said. "Just let me take these to Anita and Bristol. When they're finished, I'll go ahead and lock up."

Jan nodded eagerly and Elaine ducked back into the parlor with her prize. After thanking Bristol profusely for the information, she checked them out at the cash register, wished them a good afternoon, and bolted the front door.

Jan ducked into the hall. "Is everyone gone?"

"Yep."

Archie appeared next to her, his head swinging back and forth as he eyed Jan and then Elaine. "What is going on?"

"Archie! I'm glad you're back. Did you and Gloria finish packing?"

He nodded. "All done. We leave in the morning. I just came back to get the painting."

Elaine peeked down the hall and across the parlor. "Where is Rose?"

"Already gone for the day," Archie said, coming fully into the hall. "She had a meeting with one of her culinary professors."

"Okay." Elaine paced the floor while she filled Archie in on their visit with Trooper Benson and then what she'd learned from Bristol.

"Henry Philpott works for a mining company?" Archie's brow furrowed with confusion.

Jan's eyes narrowed. "That would explain all the maps."

"And why he knows so much about Lancaster," Elaine added. Her gaze drifted from Jan to Archie. "I think it's pretty safe to say we can cross him off our list of suspects, wouldn't you?"

Jan fell silent. After a moment, she nodded. Archie did too.

"Good, then we're agreed. So who does that leave?" Elaine held up one finger. "Bedrich Jagr is the most suspicious, in my opinion. We know for certain he's hiding at least one secret. Personally, I think he's hiding many."

Archie frowned. "Which secret is that?"

"What he's doing here, for starters, and why he's desperate enough to make threats against me."

"I don't know, Elaine." Jan's brow puckered with worry. "We can't forget about Irina. She came back in here looking for something, remember? And then there's Matthew as well. I don't think we can cross him off our list until we figure out his line of work."

"*Hmm.* You're right, I suppose." She thought for a moment. "Although I think it's safe to assume he's a security guard. Dan told us he's not a police officer."

"True. So in that case, what do you think he was doing the night Bob and I followed him from the restaurant?"

"Maybe checking on the homes of his customers?"

Jan thought a moment. "That's pretty extreme, wouldn't you say? I've never known a security company to go to such lengths for their customers. Besides, I still think we shouldn't rule him or Irina out just yet, at least until we know why Irina was faking an accent, and until we pinpoint for certain what Matthew was doing driving around."

Elaine considered this for a moment. She had to concede that Bedrich's manner had prejudiced her against him, but she couldn't let that cloud her judgment. "You have a point. If there's one thing I've learned solving all these mysteries, it's that we should never take anything for granted, no matter how small or seemingly insignificant."

"Precisely." Jan's frown deepened. "So then, what should we do?"

Elaine scratched her head. "I say we talk to Irina. We know where to find her, after all."

"The play rehearsals?" Archie asked. "Are they conducting them at the Community Opera House in Waterville?"

"That's right." Elaine waved toward the office. "I think we can find out what time the rehearsals are just by doing a quick Internet search."

She started toward the computer in their office. Jan followed close behind, but Archie stood where they'd left him, his phone in hand, staring at the screen.

"Archie, are you coming?" Jan asked.

He lifted the phone. "I'll be there in a moment. I just realized I have several unopened e-mails. I'm going to look through them, just in case one of them is from that gun expert I told you about."

Elaine and Jan nodded their agreement and then continued to the office. As Elaine had hoped, it was easy to find information on the theater where Maxwell Fisher was producing his play, but a few minutes of careful searching did not reveal the hours the cast rehearsed.

Jan adjusted her glasses. "We could call the theater and ask, I suppose. Would you like me to do it?"

Elaine pushed the phone toward her. In just a few moments, Jan was able to pinpoint the rehearsal hours at the theater, Tuesday through Friday each week, so the two of them picked up their coats and prepared to leave.

Elaine glanced at the clock and calculated the amount of time it would take for them to drive to Waterville. "Maybe if we get there early enough, we can speak to Irina before the rehearsal starts."

"Definitely." Jan poked her arms into her coat and snugged the collar. "From what I know of Maxwell Fisher, he doesn't seem the type to take kindly to someone interrupting his practice."

"Let's get a move on then, before it gets too late," Elaine said. She followed Jan to the door and clicked off the light. Archie caught them in the hall, his cell phone held high above his head.

"Elaine! Jan! Before you go, you must hear this."

Elaine pressed her hand over her heart to calm its wild pounding. "Goodness, Archie. You nearly gave me a heart attack."

"Me too," Jan said. "What are you so excited about?"

"Did you get a message from the gun expert?" Elaine asked.

"Indeed I did," he said, "and you're never going to believe what he told me."

"Well, don't keep us in suspense," Jan scolded, bracing her hands on her hips. "What did he say?"

Archie twisted the phone so they could see the message. "He said the gun isn't real. The gun we found here in the tearoom, the one we thought was used in the break-ins?" He looked from Jan to Elaine, his eyes wide and incredulous. "It's a fake."

CHAPTER TWENTY-TWO

A fake!" Jan held the phone closer to stare at the message. "But that can't be right. He must have looked at the picture wrong, or maybe it was blurry, or..."

Archie shook his head as she spoke. "I'm afraid he's not wrong, Jan. He was quite adamant in his assessment. Read what he said."

Jan scrolled through the e-mail until she got to the body of the message. "Here it is."

"Read it out loud, Jan," Elaine urged.

Jan cleared her throat nervously. "It says, *Archie, I'm so glad to hear from you...*"

Elaine fluttered her hand at Jan. "Skip that part. What did he say about the gun?"

Jan swiped up with her finger and continued reading. "*The photo you sent me is actually a picture of a very nice stage prop. Kimar, the manufacturer whose name is engraved on the side, is a company founded in 1992 by a couple of brothers who specialize in high-quality blank pistols. This gun is a replica of a popular Czech handgun, the CZ-75. Models like this one have been most widely used for stage and screen productions that feature bad guys from Eastern European countries or police forces like the Russian Federation or Czech Republic.*"

Here, Jan looked over her glasses at Elaine. "Didn't that article we read on Maxwell Fisher say he was directing a play called *Red Princess?*"

Elaine nodded slowly. "Something about Leonid Brezhnev's granddaughter."

"Yes," Archie said. "I remember seeing it in the paper."

Jan ducked her head and finished reading. "*While this gun is a fake, it's not a cheap one. Whoever purchased it wanted something that looked and felt authentic. I have to admit, I'm curious how this thing ended up in your bosses' tearoom. If you find out, be sure to let me know.*"

The e-mail finished with all the typical well wishes, which Jan did not bother to read. Stunned, she handed the phone back to Archie. "I can't believe it. The gun was a fake."

"Why didn't Dan say something? Surely he could tell the gun wasn't real," Elaine said.

"Maybe he didn't want to say anything until he was certain," Jan suggested.

"Or possibly he *knew* it was a fake"—Archie's gaze darted from Jan to Elaine and back—"but he still suspected that the gun was the one used in the break-ins. It certainly would have made a handy deterrent against any unwary homeowners who stumbled into the house at an inopportune moment."

"One thing is certain, we'll have to rethink our suspicions about Bedrich and Pasha. If this *was* the gun used in the break-ins, it eliminates Pasha as a suspect because he still had his gun when I saw him at the cottage. If it was a different weapon, it sort of clears Bedrich since it wouldn't exactly make sense for him to hire a bodyguard with a fake gun." Elaine looked shocked too, and more than a little disappointed.

"I guess not," Jan said uncertainly. She had to admit, while she had never been as convinced of Bedrich's guilt as Elaine, this sudden turn of events did surprise her. She jerked her head toward the clock on the parlor wall. "Elaine, look at the time. I definitely think we should talk to Irina and Matthew, but we'll have to hurry if we want to get to the theater before their rehearsal starts."

Elaine gasped and hurried toward the door. "You're right. Thank you for checking with your friend, Archie," she called over her shoulder.

Even though she was excited and anxious to learn what Irina and Matthew had to say about the gun, Jan drove carefully to the theater. A light rain had begun to fall. Mixed with the wet leaves gathering on the streets and along the gutters, she knew the roads would be slippery. Still, it didn't take long to pull into the parking lot of the Community Opera House. Several cars filled the parking slots, many mostly older models, but scattered among them were one or two that Jan recognized as expensive brands. Who did those belong to?

Off to the side of the building, the stage door stood open. Jan and Elaine veered that way. Inside the theater, several people crowded around the door talking and laughing. A few looked up at Jan and Elaine's entrance, but most went back to their conversations when they realized that they were of no interest.

To their left, a short flight of steps led up to the stage. On the right was another flight that went down to a door labeled Dressing Rooms.

Jan scanned the group at the entrance. Though there were a couple of faces she recognized, Irina's and Matthew's were not among them. She pressed tightly to Elaine's side, her hand gripping her elbow.

"Do you see them?" Elaine whispered.

Jan shook her head and pointed toward the stairs. "Should we check the dressing rooms?"

"Good idea."

Elaine started toward the stairs, dragging Jan with her.

"Act casual," she said as she reached for the handrail and started down the stairs. Jan did her best to imitate Elaine's straight back and slightly tilted chin, but she couldn't help looking over her shoulder, certain that at any minute, one of those people would wonder where they were going and what they were doing at the theater. Instead, they made it to the bottom of the stairs without drawing a single glance.

Voices carried from one of the dressing rooms. Jan stuck her head around the corner of the door to risk a peek. Irina paced the floor, one hand waving as she recited lines to Matthew, who leaned against the makeup counter, following along in the script.

"She's pretty good," Elaine whispered after a moment.

Jan shushed her, but it was too late. Their movements caught Irina's eye. She dropped her hand to her side and turned to look at them.

"Who are you?" she asked, in very precise, clipped syllables.

The accent was back, Jan noted, strong but distinguishable.

Matthew looked up from the script. Spotting them, he straightened and eased out to stand protectively in front of Irina. "Can I help you, ladies?"

Jan gulped as a sudden wave of stage fright overtook her. What was she doing? Why hadn't she considered what she would say? She could hardly walk up to them, a couple of complete strangers, and say, *Hello. My name is Jan. I own the Tea for Two tearoom along with my cousin here, and we were just wondering—did you happen to leave a fake gun there last week?*

Next to her, Elaine eased to the forefront, her hand outstretched. "Hello. My name is Elaine Cook." She shook hands with both Matthew and Irina and then jabbed her thumb toward Jan. "This is my cousin, Jan Blake. We own the Tea for Two tearoom in Lancaster."

Irina's eyes narrowed. "I remember that place." She looked at Matthew. "It is the large Victorian house near the lake."

Again, she leaned heavily on the accent. Maybe Jan *was* on to something. Maybe Irina did have something to hide. She studied her face carefully for signs of nervousness or guilt—a nervous twitching of her eyelids, or a reluctance to make eye contact.

Irina met her gaze steadily.

"Yes, that's the one," Elaine said. Her smile looked like something Archie's father had painted on with a paintbrush. "Jan and I were just wondering…"

Jan held her breath. *She wouldn't.*

"…since we saw you both there last week…"

She couldn't! Jan resisted the urge to cringe and cover her eyes.

"…did either of you happen to leave a gun in the tearoom?"

CHAPTER TWENTY-THREE

Elaine could almost feel the mortification rolling off her cousin. Bluntness was certainly not a tactic Jan would have employed, but Elaine knew that sometimes the direct approach worked like a battering ram, knocking a person off kilter and prohibiting them from the time it took to concoct a lie.

Matthew stepped toward them, his face hard, eyes narrowed and unreadable.

Elaine gulped. Then again, sometimes the direct approach backfired.

Jan's fingers wrapped around Elaine's arm tightly. Still, Elaine was proud that Jan held her ground.

"You found my gun?" was all Matthew said. "I had just purchased it from a pawn broker. It's for a play we're doing here at the theater called…"

"*Red Princess.* I know." Elaine crossed her arms over her chest. "You say you purchased the gun from a pawn shop? Do you know which one?"

Matthew's brows bunched together. "It's just a small place in downtown Waterville. Chester's, I think?"

"And you say you bought the gun the day you came into the tearoom?" Elaine continued.

"That's right." He swiped a lock of hair from his forehead. "Say, can one of you tell me what all of this is about? Why do I suddenly feel like I'm being interrogated?"

Elaine looked at Jan, who nodded. She turned her gaze back to Matthew and Irina. "Were either of you aware that a similar type of gun has been used in the string of break-ins that have troubled residents in Lancaster lately?"

Irina grabbed Matthew's hand in a move that spoke both intimacy and reliance. "That cannot be."

"I'm afraid it is. We saw a picture of the gun in the newspaper," Jan said.

Irina's face grew pale as she tilted her head to stare up at Matthew. "I told you we should have checked out that pawnbroker." She looked back at Elaine. "We heard about the break-ins, of course, but we didn't have anything to do them. We bought the gun to use in the play. I was the one who left it in the tearoom. It was an accident. Matthew had nothing to do with it."

This time when Irina spoke, there was no hint of an accent. She peered at them earnestly, her eyes wide and pleading. She certainly appeared guileless, but Elaine needed to be certain.

"You probably should explain that to the police," she said quietly.

"You turned it in to the police?" Consternation grew on Matthew's face.

"I'm afraid we had to," Jan said. "We had no idea the gun was a fake or who it belonged to. We certainly couldn't keep it at the tearoom."

"Of course not." Irina's fingertips turned white where she gripped Matthew's hand. "You don't think we'll be in any trouble, do you? It's not against the law to carry around a prop gun, is it?"

"To be honest, I have no idea," Elaine said. "I don't think there's any law against it, but if the gun really was used in the robberies, you may have a problem. You should check with Trooper Dan Benson, just to be sure."

"I never should have taken that thing into the tearoom with us," Matthew growled. "I should have known better and just left it in the car."

Irina shook her head. "No, it's my fault. If we hadn't been fighting, you never would have run off and left it."

Elaine and Jan shared a quick glance. So it *was* a fight they had witnessed. And Irina said he'd left it? Hadn't she just said it was she who'd left the gun?

Elaine cleared her throat and drew their attention back to her. "If you don't mind me asking, is the gun the item you were looking for when you came back to the tearoom?"

Irina nodded, wide-eyed. "We actually stopped at several places, but the last place I remembered having the bag was at your tearoom."

"Why didn't you just ask if we'd seen it?" Jan asked.

Irina shrugged. "I was in a hurry. I was headed to practice, and Maxwell gets very fidgety when we walk in late."

Elaine did a quick calculation in her head. Irina had come into the tearoom looking for the gun on Wednesday. And as Jan had discovered earlier that evening, the cast always rehearsed Tuesday through Friday. Irina's story made sense, except for one thing—her accent.

Elaine gestured toward her mouth. "You don't have an accent, do you?"

Irina stared at her blankly.

"The first time you came into the tearoom, I thought I heard an accent."

The confusion cleared from her face, replaced by chagrin. "Oh, that. To be honest, that's what Matthew and I were arguing about when we left the prop gun."

"You were arguing about an accent?" Jan frowned. "I've heard of people playing pranks and pretending to have an accent, but I've never heard of anyone arguing over one."

"Irina is very dedicated to her craft," Matthew said.

"Maybe *too* dedicated," she said quietly, looking at him with love and remorse in her eyes.

Tenderness overtook his features as he smiled back at her. He looked at Jan and Elaine and shrugged. "When Irina is studying for a character, she completely adopts their mannerisms, dialect, everything. It's 24/7 with her. She *becomes* the person she is trying to portray."

"Matthew worries that such single-minded devotion isn't healthy. We've argued about it before and we were talking about it again that day."

"You two are a couple?" Elaine asked.

They nodded together.

"It hasn't been easy because our work often takes us in different directions," Irina said, "but I know Matthew is the man for me. I just need to find a way to be devoted to my career without shutting him out."

"And I need to find a way to be more supportive of your passion," Matthew replied.

He slipped his arm around her shoulders and pulled her tight to his side. Elaine looked away, but she noted that Jan watched them with tears in her eyes.

Lord, please help my sweet cousin get through this parting with Bob. It wasn't a long prayer, but it came from the very depths of Elaine's heart.

Irina glanced apologetically at Elaine. "I'm sorry I ran out without saying anything to you. I can understand how that might have looked suspicious."

A female voice echoed down the stairs. "Irina? Matthew? Are you down there? Maxwell is looking for you."

"Tell him we're coming," Matthew called back. He tugged Irina's hand. "We should go. The rehearsal is about to begin."

Irina held up one finger. "Will you go and tell Maxwell I'm on my way up? I just need one more second."

He agreed, reluctantly. Elaine saw him pause to glance back at Irina before he disappeared up the stairs.

When he was gone, Irina turned to them, her hands clasped tightly at her waist. "I will call Trooper Benson as soon as we finish up here."

"I think that would be best," Elaine said.

She sucked in a deep breath. "The only problem is...I need him to think it was me who purchased the gun, and me who left it behind in the tearoom."

"I'm not sure I understand," Jan said. "Why is that?"

Irina's gaze fell. "It was a long time ago. Matthew was very young." When she looked up, Elaine read concern in her eyes, but not for herself. For Matthew.

"He ran into a little trouble when he was a teenager. It's followed him ever since. If that gun we bought from the pawn-broker is tied to something illegal. Well, I wouldn't want this to ruin things for him now, you know what I mean?"

"I do," Elaine said, "but lying will only make things worse. Be honest with the police. Tell them exactly what happened. Things will sort themselves out."

After a long moment, Irina nodded slowly.

"Oh, and before we forget..." Jan motioned toward Elaine and pointed toward her shoulder.

"That's right." Elaine's eyes widened and she turned to Irina. "Would you mind telling us if Matthew is a security guard?"

Irina looked confused by the question, but she nodded. "He works nights at an office building in Waterville. It was the only thing he could find that fit with our rehearsal schedule. Why?"

Jan stepped forward. "The other night, a friend and I saw him at one of the local restaurants. I wondered about his uniform, that's all." She paused, thinking. Why was Matthew driving around Lancaster if he worked in an office building in Waterville? "You say he works in Waterville?"

Irina shrugged. "Well, mostly in Waterville. The com-pany he works for has been giving him a lot of extra hours because of the break-ins. This week, he's been mostly driving—you know—checking on all of the places the security company protects."

Jan nodded. "That makes sense. Thank you."

Suddenly, Irina seemed to remember she was needed onstage. She thanked them hastily and bade them good-bye before following Matthew up the stairs.

Next to her, Jan blew out an unsteady breath. "Whew. That was a lot to take in. What do you think?"

Elaine shrugged. "We'll have to leave it to the police to determine for sure, I suppose."

"Hmm." Jan pursed her lips.

"What?"

She reached out to grip the handrail. "C'mon, Elaine. I want to get home before it gets too late." She started up the stairs. "Maybe we should call…"

She stopped so suddenly, Elaine nearly bumped into her backside. "What in the world? Jan, what are you doing?"

Slowly, Jan turned, her eyes wide with disbelief. Elaine stared up at her. She knew that look.

"You've thought of something."

Jan nodded.

"What is it?" She waited and then prompted her again. "Jan?"

Jan backed down the steps until she and Elaine stood eye to eye. "Matthew and Irina left the gun we found in the tearoom. Verifying when and where he purchased it will be easy enough, so I think it's safe to assume he's telling the truth about that part."

"Okay," Elaine said hesitantly.

Jan's hands shook as her enthusiasm grew. "That means the gun *we* found probably isn't the one used in the robberies, but another one similar to it was." She waited while Elaine processed this and knew the exact moment when Elaine realized her point. The confusion cleared from her face and she nodded.

"Pasha," Elaine said.

Jan smiled. "Yep. Pasha."

CHAPTER TWENTY-FOUR

Jan's heart pounded with excitement. They were on to something, she could feel it. She grasped Elaine's arm. "C'mon, let's get outside where we can talk."

The two hurried from the theater and climbed into Jan's car. She turned it on and flipped the heater to high. "Okay, so how about we go back over the clues?"

"Good idea." Elaine rubbed her hands together as she settled into the seat. "We've already talked about the gun, so let's start with the addresses."

Jan's brow puckered as she concentrated. "Really, the only thing they all have in common is the first two numbers. Why do you suppose that is?"

"A partial address," Elaine reiterated, pinching her lower lip. "A partial address, a common airport—of course, we have no idea which airport Bedrich used—a rare gun..."

Jan reached out and grabbed her arm. "Elaine, wait. Let's think about this a moment. Where would you see addresses in an airport?"

"Maybe on a baggage claim ticket or—a luggage tag!"

Jan nodded, her thoughts racing now. "A luggage tag, right. So if a person only caught a glimpse of the address on a luggage tag…"

"But why would they be looking at someone else's luggage?"

"Maybe it was similar?" She wound her finger in a circle in the air. "I've often mistaken my luggage for someone else's on those carousel things."

Elaine drummed her hand on the dash. "Yes, you're right. So maybe if two bags got mixed up…"

"And something got placed into the wrong bag…"

"But the person realized it before the other bag left the airport and they caught a glimpse of the address…"

"But they couldn't claim the other person's bag because something inside was stolen…"

"The stamps!" they exclaimed in unison.

For the space of a full second, they simply stared at one another. Jan blew out a sigh.

"All right, so we may have figured out the how and why, but we still cannot be one hundred percent certain of the who."

"We have a pretty good idea though," Elaine said, leaning back against her seat.

Jan agreed. "I think we should pay a visit to our friend Mr. Jagr, although it might be a good idea to let Dan know what we've uncovered."

Elaine pulled her phone from her purse. There was a *beep, beep, beep* as she dialed the numbers, and then she pressed the phone to her ear and waited. After a moment, she said, "Hello, Dan. This is Elaine Cook."

Briefly, Elaine summed up what they knew and then asked that the trooper call before she hung up.

Jan scowled and drummed her fingers against the steering wheel. "No answer?"

"Uh-uh." Elaine bit her lip nervously. "I don't know, Jan. I don't feel good about delaying. Something tells me we should get over to Jagr's place and see what we can find out."

The screen on her phone darkened, casting the interior of the car into shadow once again. The minutes ticked by, but when the trooper still had not called, Jan put the car into Drive and pulled on to the highway.

Elaine lifted her eyebrow and Jan shrugged. "Don't put off until tomorrow what you can do today."

Elaine chuckled. "Or as Nana used to say, don't stand around watching the milk curdle." A mile passed, and then another. Elaine pointed to a sign up ahead that advertised Lake Country Cottages. Jan nodded and turned on to Cottage Road. There were fewer campers than there had been earlier that summer, and fewer people gathered around campfires. The ones that remained huddled in blankets or donned hoodies to ward off the chill. It wouldn't be long, Jan thought, before Lancaster and Penzance returned to hibernation right along with most of the tourists.

"There it is." Elaine pointed up ahead, where the glow of the headlamps just caught the edge of the driveway. She leaned forward on the seat. "Looks like something is going on."

Jan slowed. "It sure does. What are all those police cars doing there?"

"Police cars? Are you sure?"

Elaine clutched the dashboard as she strained to see. Jan crawled to a stop and pointed out the passenger side window.

"Look there. That's Trooper Benson's SUV."

They watched quietly for a moment, but though there were multiple cars with flashing lights, there was very little activity.

"We should go," Elaine whispered.

Jan readily agreed. She turned the car back toward the tearoom. The house with its brightly glowing porch lights was a welcome sight. Jan parked the car and then followed Elaine inside.

Elaine flipped on the light in the office and then set down her things on the desk. "What do you suppose was going on?"

"I have no idea." She grimaced. "I hope it wasn't an accident."

Though they undoubtedly wondered if the police presence had anything to do with Bedrich Jagr, neither of them said a word as they proceeded to the kitchen. Jan put a kettle on to boil and Elaine fetched the cups.

While they waited for the water to heat, Elaine paced the floor. Jan watched her from the kitchen table. Finally, when she could stand it no longer, she pushed out a chair.

"Elaine, come sit down." She waited until her cousin complied before looking her squarely in the eyes. "We probably won't know anything about that until tomorrow morning, so there's no sense worrying."

"You're right." Elaine sighed and dropped her gaze, her left thumb flicking the nail on her right. "There is something else

I've been meaning to talk to you about. We've just been too busy for me to actually do it."

Jan rested her hands against the tabletop. "All right then, what about now?"

Elaine nodded. "Yes, I think now is a good time." She sucked in a deep breath. "You know Archie is taking the painting to the person Nathan recommended to get it authenticated."

"Of course. They're going to New York. He and Gloria are planning to make a vacation out of it."

"Exactly. But what we haven't talked about is what we'll do after."

Jan shook her head in confusion. "After?"

She made a rolling motion with her hand. "After it's authenticated, I mean. Will we sell the painting to Archie or simply give it to him? And if it turns out to be valuable, then what?"

"Yes, we'll need to talk about it." Jan rubbed her eyes, suddenly wearier than she'd been in months. "But not tonight, okay? I have too much on my mind already, and I still have to finish making the arrangements for Bob's party."

"Okay," Elaine said hesitantly. She placed her hand on Jan's shoulder. "Can I help? I can take over the party planning, if you'd like."

Jan pushed up from the table and motioned to the stove. "Actually, I think it will do me good to get my thoughts on something productive. I may even whip up a batch of Bob's favorite cookies." She gave Elaine's hand a pat. "Give him something to remember me by."

Elaine gave a knowing smile. She puttered about the kitchen for a bit but finally agreed to leave Jan to her party preparations after Jan insisted she would be fine. Jan sighed as the kitchen door swung closed behind Elaine. So much change ahead. It was never easy. Many times, change was just plain hard. But she needed to be prepared for it—needed to trust that no matter what God had in store, it would all work out in the end.

CHAPTER TWENTY-FIVE

Saturday morning, Elaine lingered outside Jan's bedroom door. Should she knock? Jan's light had stayed on well into the night hours, long after Elaine had gone to bed. More than likely she was just catching up on some much-needed sleep.

Downstairs Elaine heard the doorbell chime. She let her hand fall to her side and went to answer. Priscilla waved to her through the glass and Elaine opened the door.

"Good morning, Elaine. I know it's early. I hope you don't mind that I stopped by."

"Not at all, Priscilla." Elaine opened the door wider. "Come in."

"Thank you."

Elaine motioned toward the kitchen. "I was just about to make myself a pot of coffee. Would you like some?"

Priscilla's smile was hesitant. "If it's not too much trouble."

"Not at all. Like I said, I was going to make some for myself anyway. Jan prefers tea, but I need something a little stronger in the morning sometimes. Come on back."

Elaine led the way, her slippered feet making a soft scuffling sound on the floor. "What has you out and about so early in the morning?" she asked as they entered the kitchen. She waved toward one of the chairs, inviting Priscilla to sit.

"Actually, I was hoping to see you."

"Oh?" Elaine reached for the coffee tin and prepared the filter while Priscilla claimed a seat at the table.

"It's about what you said, you know, about being open to dating." She ducked her head, hiding her face, but the flush creeping up her neck gave away her emotions as surely as if she'd looked Elaine in the eye. Elaine was honored that Priscilla had opened up to her in this way. She'd hoped to become closer friends with Priscilla for some time now, and the vulnerability Priscilla was showing with her felt like a small breakthrough.

Elaine smiled as she filled the pot with water. "Did Curtis ask you out?"

Priscilla's eyes widened. "How did you guess?"

Elaine laughed. "Well, his attraction was pretty obvious."

"Oh." She sighed. "Obvious to everyone but me, I guess. Anyway, we went out for dinner. Afterward, he suggested we go to a movie."

"That's wonderful," Elaine said, taking two cups out of the cupboard and setting them next to the coffeemaker. The pleasing aroma of coffee had begun to waft through the kitchen, but Priscilla seemed not to notice as she rubbed her hands over her face.

"Actually, I didn't go."

"What? Why not?" Elaine sat down next to Priscilla and softened her tone. "Don't you like him?"

Uncertainty welled in Priscilla's eyes.

"Oh," Elaine whispered. "I see." She floundered for something comforting to say, something that wouldn't sound condescending. "He likes you, right?"

Priscilla blushed. "I think so."

"That's a good thing." Remembering their last conversation, Elaine lowered her head to peer into Priscilla's eyes. "Did you tell him about Charles?"

"I started to, but..." She shook her head.

Elaine laid her palms against the table. "Priscilla, do you mind if I ask why you're so hesitant?"

"I asked myself the same question." She blew out a shuddering breath. "Elaine, when a person is younger, it's expected that they will dream of finding that one special person to share their life with. I wanted a home and a family, a husband to grow old with, just like everyone else. But then Charles died, and the years passed, and I sort of reconciled myself to the idea that I might never marry. I wasn't sad about that," she added quickly. "God calls some people to remain single, and I thought maybe that would be true of me."

"But that changed?" Elaine asked.

"Maybe. I'm not sure. See, it *was* hard at first, but eventually I learned to take care of myself. I was independent."

"But?" Elaine prompted. Though Priscilla spoke the words proudly, she sensed there was more struggling to come out.

Her shoulders slumped. "Then my house was broken into. All of a sudden, I was scared, and tired of being alone...and Curtis was there." She wrung the words out one by one.

"But you knew that being lonely wasn't a good enough reason to date someone."

She shook her head sadly. "No."

"Is that why you refused to go out with him?"

"That's the problem," she said, throwing her hands up in frustration. "I'm not sure. I like Curtis. He's a nice person. But dating is about more than just *liking*, isn't it? I don't have those kinds of feelings for him."

The words pricked Elaine's heart. Her feelings for Nathan went much deeper than a desire for companionship. She loved him. And she owed it to him to explain that she'd been trying to protect him by not telling him about her concern for Ben's reputation.

"Then there's only one thing for you to do, isn't there?" she asked quietly.

Priscilla stared at her in confusion.

Elaine cleared her throat and spoke up. "Priscilla, you're going to have to be completely honest with Curtis. Tell him you value his friendship but nothing more."

She clasped Priscilla's hand and hoped she conveyed with that touch how well she understood.

"But don't close yourself off to the possibility of romance. And remember, if you really want to find someone, you're going to have to open up the secret places in your heart and invite people in. The man God wants for you won't ask you to change who you are. That man will just soak up a little of that hurt and loneliness you've been hiding and replace them with joy and love."

Elaine leaned forward, drawing Priscilla's gaze. "But you'll also do the same for him. He has to be willing to open up just as much as you are."

"You're right," she whispered. She blinked several times, and then gave Elaine's fingers a squeeze. "I knew you were the right person to talk to. My life before the break-in was comfortable. Safe. Now, I feel so shaken. I just don't know…"

Elaine gave her hand a pat. "None of us knows, Priscilla. That's the beauty of it. Life is unpredictable, but having someone to share it with makes the unpredictability something to cherish instead of fear." She smiled. "A good man would want you to be honest with him, even if that means taking things slow until you can be sure of what you feel in your heart."

Saying the words out loud was strangely comforting. Elaine knew now why she had been hesitant to tell Nathan about Bedrich's threats against Ben. It was because deep down, she was still holding on to a special place that was reserved only for her first love.

But she loved Nathan too.

Somehow, she would continue to find a way to reconcile both of those truths in her heart.

Footsteps sounded on the stairs, and she and Priscilla looked up to see Jan enter the kitchen. She was fully dressed, her hair and makeup neat, but there were circles under her eyes, and Elaine knew her suspicions about Jan's lack of sleep were correct.

"Good morning," Jan said. Her smile was too bright, her attempt at cheerfulness too forced.

Elaine and Priscilla responded with a quiet "good morning" and then Elaine pointed to the coffeemaker. "I didn't bother with tea, but the coffee is almost ready if you would like some."

To her surprise, Jan nodded and took down a cup from the shelf. She rarely drank anything but tea.

Priscilla looked from Jan to Elaine hesitantly. "Well, I should probably get going."

Jan picked up one of the empty cups on the counter. "But you haven't had your coffee yet, have you?"

"No, but I'm sure you and Elaine need to get the tearoom ready to open, and I don't want to get in your way."

Jan lowered the cup slowly. "Actually, I wouldn't mind the company. Would you, Elaine?"

"Not at all." Elaine got up to fill their cups and carried one back to the table for Priscilla.

"Besides, I have some blueberry muffins leftover from yesterday." Jan pulled the plate from the refrigerator and set them on the table next to Priscilla's cup. "Help yourself."

Priscilla plucked one off the plate and set it on a napkin carefully. "Don't mind if I do."

"How are things at the library? Good, I hope?"

"Uh…"

"Oh dear." Jan reached up to pat her eyes and the top of her head. "I left my glasses upstairs. Would you excuse me for a moment while I…?"

The front doorbell rang before she could finish.

"Who could that be?" Jan asked.

"I'll check." Elaine rose, but Jan motioned her to sit.

"I'll do it. Go ahead and enjoy your coffee with Priscilla."

Her footsteps faded down the hall. Priscilla turned to Elaine.

"Is she okay? She looked a little tired." She pointed to her face and waved her finger in a circle.

"I know. She'll be fine. There's just a lot going on right now, and I think it's all hit her at once."

Priscilla nodded understandingly. Elaine got up and stuck her head into the hall.

"Jan, is everything okay? Who is it?"

"I think you'd better come see, Elaine," Jan replied.

Elaine looked back at Priscilla. "I'll just be a moment."

She smiled and picked up a muffin. "Take your time."

Elaine walked slowly out toward the east parlor. From this vantage point, she could just make out Jan's face. She was staring at someone, and she looked worried. No—*worried* wasn't the right word. Her eyes were wide. Her fingers were pressed to her mouth. Her skin was pale and...

She looked horrified.

CHAPTER TWENTY-SIX

Elaine crept down the hall, fear building in her chest with every step. "Jan?" Her voice came out a raspy squeak. She swallowed and tried again. "Are you all right?"

Jan lowered her hand from her mouth to beckon. "Come in, Elaine. It's Dan. You need to hear this."

With the mention of Dan's name, Elaine immediately felt a bit of the tension drain from her shoulders.

"Goodness, Jan, you gave me a fright."

She trailed off as she entered the parlor. No wonder Jan had looked so solemn. Dan was in uniform, his hat in one hand as he peered at them gravely. The other hand was bandaged heavily and his left eye, though not blackened, definitely looked red and swollen.

"Dan! My goodness, what happened? What's wrong?"

"I have some news." He motioned toward one of the tables with his hat. "Maybe we should sit down."

Once they were seated, Dan laid his hat on the table and clasped his hands. "I have to thank you both for your help in the investigation regarding the break-ins around Lancaster."

"You caught the person behind them?"

He gave a curt nod. "Thanks to the two of you."

"Us?" Elaine and Jan shared a glance.

"So you got my message last night about the gun belonging to Matthew and Irina?" Elaine asked.

"I did, and that only helped solidify the clues you'd already given us." Dan reached into his pocket and took out his notepad. "Thanks to your tip on the addresses, we were able to figure out which houses around Lancaster would likely be targeted. Last night, we set up a stakeout. Your hunch was right about Jagr. He's not a diplomat. In fact, his name isn't Jagr. It's Hubert Dvorak."

He laid down his notepad to rest his arms against the table. "You were right about the connection between the victims of the robberies. They all had the number eighty-one in their address."

"What about Pasha?" Elaine lifted her eyebrows. "Did he have a fake name too?"

"Oddly enough, no. His name really is Pasha. His last name is Novotny. He's a petty thief back in his home country, with just a few minor offenses on his rap sheet." He lifted his injured hand and pointed to his eye. "That will likely change now though."

Elaine let out a small gasp. "Is that what happened to your hand?"

He nodded. "We apprehended Novotny at the stakeout, but not without a fight. Another team went to the cottages for his partner."

"We saw the lights," Jan said, pressing her hand atop Elaine's. "That must be what we saw when we drove by."

"Around nine thirty?" he asked.

Jan nodded.

"More than likely, you drove past just as we were wrapping up," he said. "Unfortunately, Dvorak is still on the loose, which is why I came by today. I wanted you both to be aware and on the lookout in case he shows up again."

"But we didn't travel," Elaine said. "Why would he come here?"

Dan smiled. "Because you're the reason we were on to him in the first place, although he may not know that for certain." He took out his phone and pulled up a photo, then turned it for Jan and Elaine to see. "Remember these?"

"The stamps!" they exclaimed together.

He pulled his phone back. "Exactly. It turns out Dvorak is the major suspect in their disappearance. Officials from that country followed him to the United States, but he was able to escape them before they could track him here to Lancaster."

"Excuse me." Priscilla peeked into the parlor, one hand lifted in apology. "I'm so sorry. I couldn't help but overhear."

Elaine jumped to her feet and pulled Priscilla into the parlor. "Gracious, I forgot all about leaving you in the kitchen. I'm so sorry."

She turned to Dan, who rose to greet Priscilla with a handshake. "Trooper Benson, you remember Priscilla Gates?"

"Of course. Good morning, Miss Gates."

"I'm so sorry to interrupt." Priscilla said. "I thought I heard you mention something about the break-ins?"

"That's correct." He motioned toward the table. "Please join us. This involves you too, since you were one of the first to have your home broken into."

When they were all seated, he resumed where he'd left off.

"Hubert Dvorak masterminded the idea to steal those rare stamps and smuggle them into this country with the aid of an old friend, Pasha Novotny. Unfortunately for them, they didn't get very far before the Czech authorities figured out who was behind the theft. According to Novotny, officials followed them to Augusta, where Dvorak spotted them and ditched the stamps before they could be caught."

"Ditched them where?" Elaine began, and then held up her hand. "Wait, the suitcases. He shoved them into someone else's bag?"

Dan tapped his temple. "Good thinking, Elaine. That's exactly what he did. Novotny took a picture of the luggage tag. Unfortunately, he only had time for one hasty shot, and it wasn't very good. He and Dvorak only got a piece of the information—a partial address and the name of the town."

"Lancaster," Jan said.

"So he came here looking for the stamps?" Priscilla's hand rose to her mouth. "That's why he broke into my house? And why he might come back?"

Dan nodded. "We think so. You don't have to worry, however. He's already checked your place once. I doubt…"

Priscilla cut him off with a shake of her head. "You don't understand." Her hands shook as she pushed up from the table. "He didn't look in my suitcases, and I haven't unpacked. After the break-in, I just shoved that suitcase into the laundry room and left it. I kept meaning to empty the clothes into the bin, but then I had to file a police report, and look at security systems, and I just never got around to it."

Elaine gaped at her as a thought struck. "What if the stamps really are in your bag? What if the only reason Bedrich—I mean Dvorak—didn't find them is because he was interrupted before he could search your suitcase?"

Priscilla's face paled as she nodded. "I need to get home."

Dan stood with her and pulled out his phone. "Are you all right to drive?"

She nodded. "Of course."

"Then head home but don't touch the suitcase. I'll have an officer meet you there."

"Thank you."

Elaine followed Priscilla to the door and gave her a hug.

She squeezed Elaine back and then slipped outside. Elaine closed the door behind her and returned to the parlor.

"What now, Dan?" she heard Jan ask. "Do we just wait until Dvorak is found?"

"I'm afraid so," he replied. "But at least we know what kind of vehicle he's driving. On last report, he was said to have been spotted heading toward Waterville. I think it's only a matter of time until we catch up to him."

"There's still one thing I don't understand," Elaine said, retaking her seat. She took a moment to explain the threats Bedrich had made against Ben. "He claimed to be a diplomat," she continued, "so it made sense that he was able to dig up so much information about my husband, but if he didn't have the connections he claimed, how did he know?"

Dan thought a moment and started to shrug, then stopped and pointed to a picture above the mantel. "Has that picture always been there?"

Elaine looked where he pointed. "My photo of Ben? Yes, it's always..."

Jan grabbed her hand. "Elaine, he's in uniform."

"What? Oh." She stood and walked to the fireplace. Hands trembling, she took down the picture and carried it with her back to the table. "Could it be that this was enough to give Dvorak the information he needed?"

"Maybe not just that." Jan waved her hand around the tearoom. "The picture, combined with our collection of teapots from around the world, the things we said..." She shrugged.

"He's a con artist. Those things together probably gave him enough information to draw a pretty solid conclusion about you and Ben," Dan said.

Just then, the front doorbell rang, and Jan rose quickly to answer. "I'll get it." She directed an encouraging look toward Elaine before disappearing into the hall.

Elaine rubbed her hand wearily over her face. "It's all so unbelievable. To think Dvorak concocted this entire scheme for a few thousand dollars."

"More than a few," Dan replied. "That stamp collection contained several very rare stamps. The entire thing together is probably valued at close to a million."

Her heart skipped a beat at the words. "Then there's no telling what Dvorak would have done to get his hands on them."

"No, there's not, which is why we are handling his apprehension with such care. He's dangerous, Elaine. I wouldn't take any threats he made against you lightly."

"Fortunately, they weren't against me," she said, blowing out a shaky breath. "But I certainly believed everything he said about Ben. I am beyond glad he can't carry them out."

Dan gave a slight nod. "I am too. And now, I'm going to have to leave so I can check back in with the office."

They both looked up at the sound of Nathan's voice. He entered with Jan, concern written on his face as he crossed to Elaine.

"Jan told me what happened. Are you all right?"

"We're fine," she said, "but I'm glad you're here." She gestured to Dan. "The police were able to arrest Pasha, but Bedrich—I mean Dvorak—is still on the loose."

"Then it really is a good thing I'm here." He looked at Dan. "I'll stay with them until you can track down Dvorak."

"Good." He nodded and replaced his hat on his head. "I'll be in touch as soon as we hear something."

He went to the door and let himself out. Jan locked it securely behind him, then turned to rest her back against the glass.

"Oh, Elaine, can you believe it?"

"Hardly," she said, pressing tighter against Nathan's side. A shudder shook her, and Nathan slipped his arm about her shoulders.

"Are you sure you're both all right? Tell me everything Trooper Benson said."

Jan straightened and moved down the hall toward the kitchen. "We will, but first, coffee."

Nathan glanced at Elaine in surprise and then back at Jan. "Coffee?"

"Some days require stouter stuff than tea. Luckily, Elaine has a pot already on."

She led the way to the kitchen while Elaine filled Nathan in on their conversation with Dan.

"I'm so grateful he wasn't seriously injured," she finished. "Our men in uniform take such risks for our protection. I'll have to remember to thank him again next time I see him."

Jan set a cup of coffee next to Nathan, and then took a sip of hers. She made a face and poured it down the sink. "Mine got cold sitting on the counter, and it's bad enough when it's hot." She reached into the cupboard and took out the tea tin. "You know what? I take back what I said earlier. It's *especially* the worst days that call for a soothing cup of tea."

Elaine chuckled as she refilled her own cup and went to sit next to Nathan at the table. "Thank you for coming by," she said softly. "I feel better with you here, but how did you know something was up?"

"I didn't," he admitted with a smile. "I just wanted to see you."

Elaine returned his smile and then looked at Jan. "Will you excuse us for a moment? We'll be on the porch if you need us."

Jan gave a knowing wink and waved.

Nathan grabbed his cup then placed his hand on Elaine's back and guided her outside. A gentle breeze was blowing, stirring the trees and the leaves that were just beginning to lose their summer luster. Soon they would wear a vibrant coat of orange and red.

Change. It came as surely as the seasons.

Elaine sighed and slid into one of the rocking chairs.

"Are you all right?" Nathan lowered himself into the chair next to hers.

"I am, but I'm glad you came by. We need to talk," she said. Normally she would have enjoyed a morning like this one, with the sun warm on her face but the temperatures crisp with the promise of fall. Today, her heart just felt heavy.

"Are you sure?"

Hearing the concern in his voice, she looked over at him and smiled. "I'm fine, Nathan. Truly."

He shrugged and set his cup by his feet. "Okay, then I guess I'm just wondering why you didn't tell me about Bedrich's threats." He motioned toward the house. "I overheard you talking to Dan."

The words hung between them, the implication unspoken but clear.

Don't you trust me?

"For a long time, I wasn't sure why I didn't want to tell you," she said at last.

Nathan braced his arms against his knees, his hands clasped. It was a protective move. She knew because he refused to look at her.

He cleared his throat, his head lowered. "And now?"

She took her time, forming her words carefully. When she didn't answer right away, he blew out a breath and stood.

"Elaine, are we okay? Did I do something or ...?"

"No, Nathan, it isn't that."

"Then did I say something? Because I'm really feeling like there's a wall between us, something holding us apart." He stood up and paced the porch restlessly. "Which really doesn't make any sense because as far as I'm concerned, you're the woman for me, Elaine"

Elaine got up and crossed to him. "Nathan, please listen to me."

He stopped pacing, but he didn't reach out to her. She laid her hands on his arms and felt the tension that knotted his muscles—tension she had put there simply by not being honest with him. Shame heated her face.

"Will you sit with me and give me a chance to explain?" she asked quietly. "Please?"

He didn't refuse, so she let her hand slip down his arm to clasp his hand and lead him back to the rocking chairs.

"Nathan, you are very dear to me, I hope you know that," she began. "I honestly did not expect to love anyone again after I lost Ben. For months I thought I was destined to nurse a broken heart. But then...you."

She paused to fight a rising swell of emotion, and to study the dear lines of his face. How different the two loves of her life were, and how different her feelings. But her love for Nathan was not lesser simply because it had come later. She *could* love the one just as much as the other, and if Nathan was the man she thought he was, than he would understand what needed to be said next.

"I haven't been honest with you," she whispered, hating the hurt her words sparked in Nathan's eyes. "I mean, I've tried to be but..."

His jaw hardened. "Elaine, if you're trying to tell me that you don't love me, please just say it."

She laid her hand on his cheek and smiled. "It's not that at all. In fact, it's the opposite."

He turned to her, his shoulders sagging in relief. "Then I don't understand. Why didn't you tell me?"

"Because I was worried about you."

Confusion marred his brow.

"Nathan, I love you very much. But I love Ben too," she went on quickly. "There will be times—birthdays and holidays and such—that I miss him even though I'm with you."

Though she knew the words hurt him, he didn't flinch or look away.

"Of course you love Ben. I don't expect you to forget about your feelings for him simply because you have feelings for me."

She sighed, thankful for his understanding. He looked at her with so much love and patience she wanted to fall into his arms.

"Elaine, I love you. If you need space, I'll give you that, but if you need someone close, well, I'll give you that too. Just tell me, Elaine. Tell me what you need so I can give it to you. Don't feel you have to hide it from me to spare my feelings, okay?"

She couldn't speak, so she wiped the tears from her eyes and nodded.

Noises sounded from the kitchen and Elaine realized for the first time that the window was open. Rose would be arriving soon, and then it would be time for the tearoom to open.

Normal, everyday things for a not-so-normal, everyday time.

Elaine lifted her chin. Change was good. It wasn't always easy, but it was good. And whatever lay ahead, she would embrace it with both arms.

CHAPTER TWENTY-SEVEN

Jan hovered near the window, her heart in her throat as Nathan walked down the back steps. The door opened and she spun toward Elaine. Tears wet her cousin's cheeks. Jan grabbed a handful of paper towels and rushed over to push them into Elaine's hands.

"Are you all right?"

Elaine nodded and ripped off one of the paper towels to dry her cheeks and wipe her nose. "You heard?"

"I couldn't help it. I'm sorry," Jan said.

"Don't be. It saves me from having to say everything twice." She wadded up the paper towel and tossed it into the trash. "Oh, Jan, just when I thought my heart was finally healed and I had finally dealt with my grief over losing Ben. Why now, after all these months?"

Jan rubbed Elaine's arm sadly. "Did you honestly think you would only have to deal with it once?"

Elaine froze and then slowly her shoulders slumped. "I guess that was foolish, wasn't it?"

"Not foolish. Naïve, maybe, or perhaps it was just wishful thinking."

Elaine searched the kitchen. "Where's Rose?"

"Getting the tearoom ready." Jan held up the telephone. "I just heard from Archie. He and Gloria made it to New York without any trouble. He's already met with the people Nathan recommended."

Elaine held her breath. "And?"

"Archie said they got quite excited when they saw our painting. They already believe it is by Harvey Archibald Benningham." That was Archie's father's pseudonym, they'd discovered recently. "Of course, they'll take all the proper steps to be certain, but that means he'll have to leave the painting with them to authenticate, and it could take some time."

"How much time?" Elaine asked.

Jan shrugged. "He wasn't sure."

Elaine frowned. "Was he disappointed that he won't know anything sooner?"

"Actually, he said he and Gloria are having a fantastic time," Jan said, smiling. "He's supposed to be sending us some pictures later, and he said he'd post plenty of them on Facebook."

Slowly, Jan's smile faded. Elaine crossed to her and took her hand. "Jan? What is it?"

Jan straightened and lifted her chin. "It's just that hearing you and Nathan talk, and hearing the joy in Archie's voice, I suddenly realized I've been allowing disappointment to weigh heavily on my heart, robbing me of my joy. Planning Bob's going-away party has been a chore because I'm not happy about his going. Somehow, I need to find a way to give that over to the Lord."

"That sounds like a wise plan," Elaine said with a gentle smile. "But you don't have to do that alone. Let me pray with you, and then I'll help you tackle those last-minute details for tomorrow."

Jan let her shoulders slump gratefully. "Thank you, Elaine. I could use both of those things right about now."

In fact, the preparations went much faster with Elaine working alongside her. Jan managed to make several batches of cookies while Elaine set out cups, plates, and napkins and then decorated the tearoom with a few homemade signs she made on the computer. When they finished, Jan eyed their handiwork with approval. They were all set to give Bob a nice send off tomorrow.

The next morning, Jan and Elaine hurried home from church to await their guests. Jan even knew what she would say to Bob—every word of which fled the moment she opened the door and saw him standing on their doorstep. Fortunately, their friends had already begun to arrive, so Jan invited him inside and then scurried to the kitchen to start bringing out the food.

It was a wonderful time, one Jan knew she would cherish in the months to come. Bob too seemed to enjoy himself as he chatted with friends about his plans once he reached Baltimore. By the time the last guest left and Elaine had gone upstairs to change before cleaning up, Jan was tired but happy and truly felt she'd achieved a measure of peace—except for one last thing she'd been putting off for too long.

She caught Bob's eye and motioned toward the east parlor. "Can we talk?"

He nodded and followed her in, but instead of joining her at one of the tables, he paced in front of the window. For several long moments, he said nothing, and then he turned to look at her, and resignation took over his features.

"So this is it."

She didn't ask what he meant. She knew.

"There is something I want you to know," he said slowly. "Something I'd like to say before I go." He leaned toward her, his face pinched with regret. "I was wrong to try and pull you away, Jan. You worked hard to get where you are. It's your dream, one you share with Elaine. I was wrong to ask you to give it up for me when I wasn't willing to make the same choice myself."

Listening to him, peace washed over her. She was right to speak to him, alone, one last time before saying goodbye. Even with tears burning her eyes, she knew she would have regretted doing anything less. She rose, and he stood with her.

"I'll miss you," he said. His own eyes reddened, breaking Jan's already bruised heart.

She stepped toward him, leaned in close, and pressed her lips to his cheek.

She heard him breathe in, felt his shoulders tense beneath her hands.

"I'll miss you too," she whispered.

She pushed away while she still had the strength to do so. Her knees shook as she watched him cross the room to the door. He paused, his hand resting on the knob.

"I love you, Jan."

"I love you too, Bob."

He gave her one last, long look and then opened the door and stepped through.

CHAPTER TWENTY-EIGHT

Elaine waited until lunchtime on Monday before going to see Priscilla. As she'd expected, a collection of rare stamps had been found in Priscilla's suitcase. A meeting had been set up for her to formally hand over the stamps to Czech officials, and Elaine had offered to stay with her until then.

Elaine knocked on Priscilla's front door. She could hear voices inside, but a minute or so ticked past and she was lifting her hand to knock again when the door finally opened. Priscilla waved her in, then gestured to Dan and another officer, one on the radio and the other on his cell phone.

"State troopers just apprehended Dvorak outside of Waterville," Priscilla said in a low voice. "They're still tying up loose ends, but I was about to get drinks for the officers."

"Can I help with something?" Elaine asked.

"If you'd like," Priscilla said, without meeting her gaze. She led the way into the kitchen. "Would you mind grabbing a lemon out of the refrigerator and slicing it up for tea?"

"I'd be glad to."

Elaine fetched the lemon while Priscilla took out a cutting board and knife. She also removed a small glass tray from one of the cupboards and set it next to the lemon. "Here you go. You can put the slices on that."

"Thank you." Elaine sliced carefully, watching Priscilla from the corner of her eye while she arranged the lemon on the tray. "So Dvorak is in custody and the stamps will go back to their rightful owner."

Priscilla agreed with a slight nod and continued adding ice to the pitcher.

Elaine pushed the plate of lemon aside and eased closer to her. "Priscilla, are you all right?"

Her hands stilled. "I'm fine. It's just..."

"What?"

Priscilla grimaced. "This is going to sound horribly selfish, but I'm a little sad that things will be going back to normal."

Elaine widened her eyes. "How so?"

"Well, it's just that, after I got over the trauma of having my house broken into, I realized you were right—I do need to be willing to open up more. Now that I've made that decision, I just don't want to risk settling back into my old routine."

"You don't?"

"Or maybe just not in the same way." A slow smile spread across Priscilla's face. "And I just got an idea." She reached into her pocket, pulled out her cell phone, and placed a call.

"Hello. Is this Candace Huang at the *Penzance Courier*? Oh, good. Can you make it out to my house in about ten minutes?" She gave her address. "I have a story for you about those missing Czech stamps, and how the reward for their recovery is being donated to the Lancaster Public Library for new computers. Bring a photographer. The library can use the publicity, and perhaps you'll get a scoop on a statement from the police on the case." She hung up and grinned at Elaine.

Elaine laughed and clasped Priscilla's hand. "I don't think you have to worry about the old routine, Priscilla."

"No?"

She shook her head. "Now that you've decided not to shy away from whatever the future holds, I think you'll have plenty of opportunities for adventure. In fact, I can't wait to see what God has in store."

Priscilla's eyes gleamed as she picked up the tray. "Neither can I."

It was only a matter of minutes before not only the Czech officials but the *Courier* team arrived, and Priscilla was soon staging where all the parties would stand in front of her house for the presentations, statements, and photos. Satisfied that Priscilla had the situation competently in hand and no longer needed her, Elaine said good-bye and slipped out to her car. She even hummed a tune as she drove home.

Business had indeed slowed down after Labor Day. Inside the tearoom, Rose was keeping herself busy wiping down tables and refilling the cream and sugar containers. She looked up as Elaine entered.

"You're back early. I didn't expect you until closer to one."

Elaine hung her sweater on the hall tree with a smile. "I know, but as it turns out, Priscilla didn't need my help." She told her about Dvorak's apprehension and Priscilla's actions on behalf of the library then scoured the tearoom. "Where's Jan?"

"In the kitchen." Rose paused. "Oh, and Archie asked you to call. It sounded important. Something about his father's painting, I think."

Elaine plucked her phone from her purse. "Okay. Do you know how long ago he called?"

Rose's nose scrunched. "About thirty minutes or so, I think."

"Okay. Will you let Jan know about Dvorak?"

Rose nodded and then Elaine went out onto the back porch to call Archie. He answered on the second ring.

After exchanging pleasantries, Archie cleared his throat. "I, uh, met with the woman Nathan recommended. Beatrice Miller-Pyle is her name."

"Yes, Jan told me," Elaine said. "That's wonderful, Archie. Maybe she'll even be able to tell you something about the history of the piece."

"Yes, I've thought of that. If indeed it's truly what I want."

"What do you mean? Why wouldn't it be?"

Elaine heard uncertainty in Archie's voice as he spoke. "I don't know the woman in the painting, Elaine, but I think I need to, more than I need to know why my father stopped painting. She holds the key. I sense it. And yet I fear how my life will change once I finally know the truth."

Elaine paced the length of the porch. "Fear isn't from the Lord, Archie," she said gently.

"No, it isn't."

"But it *is* okay to admit to Him what's in your heart and ask Him to help you through those feelings."

He agreed with a quiet grunt. "I'll have to leave the painting here while it's being authenticated, but once I know the truth, I'll bring it back to Lancaster and the tearoom where it belongs."

"I'm not concerned," Elaine said. "I know you'll take care of it. We'll worry about the rest when you get back."

"I can never thank you and Jan enough for this."

She dismissed his thanks with a gentle wave. "We haven't done anything, and your work has just begun."

"I suppose that is true." He chuckled. "And I suppose I had better be about it."

Elaine nodded. "You'll call again and let us know how things are going in New York?"

"I will." He hesitated for a long moment, and then she heard him sigh. "Elaine?"

"Yes, Archie?"

"That was good advice you gave me about telling God what's in my heart and letting Him help me through those feelings. Heed those words when it comes to Nathan, would you?"

A smile started in her heart and spread upward to her lips. "I intend to, Archie," she said, and knew deep down that she meant it. "I intend to."

ABOUT THE AUTHOR

Elizabeth Ludwig is an award-winning author and speaker whose books have been featured in *Southern Writers, More to Life,* and *Christian Fiction Online Magazine.* Book three in her popular Edge of Freedom series, *Tide and Tempest,* was recently named a finalist for the Gayle Wilson Award of Excellence. Elizabeth was also named a finalist in the 2015 Selah Awards for her novella "One Holy Night," part of the best-selling anthology collection *Christmas Comes to Bethlehem, Maine.* Her latest releases include *Where Hope Dwells* and *A Stitch in Time,* part of the Sugarcreek Amish Mysteries series from Guideposts. She often attends conferences and seminars where she lectures on editing for fiction writers, crafting effective novel proposals, and conducting successful editor-agent interviews. Along with her husband and children, she makes her home in the great state of Texas. To learn more, visit ElizabethLudwig.com.

Jan's Crumbly Cranberry Scones

Scones

2 cups all-purpose flour

5 tablespoons sugar

1 tablespoon baking
powder

½ teaspoon salt

6 tablespoons chilled
unsalted butter

⅔ cup (plus 1 tablespoon)
half-and-half

½ cup halved fresh
cranberries, drained on
paper towels (can substitute
dried cranberries)

1 grated zest of one orange

Preheat oven to 425 degrees. In a bowl, whisk together flour, sugar, baking powder, and salt. With a pastry blender or two knives, cut in butter until mixture forms coarse crumbs. Stir in two-thirds cup half-and-half until just moistened. Gently fold in cranberries and orange zest.

On a lightly floured surface, knead dough gently, five to ten times. Pat into a one-inch-thick round. Cut into eight wedges (like slicing a pizza) and place on a baking sheet, two inches apart. Brush tops with remaining half-and-half. Bake until golden brown, twelve to fifteen minutes. Remove from oven and cool on a wire rack. While scones are still just slightly warm, prepare the glaze.

GLAZE

2 cups powdered sugar

2 tablespoons freshly
    squeezed orange juice

1 large orange, zested

2 teaspoons pure vanilla extract

¼ teaspoon fresh nutmeg
    (more if you're a big fan of
    nutmeg!)

In a small bowl, whisk together all ingredients until smooth. If the glaze is too stiff, add another teaspoon of fresh-squeezed orange juice. Drizzle the orange-nutmeg glaze over the scones using a spoon. Allow icing to set completely, then enjoy and share.

READ ON FOR AN EXCITING SNEAK PEEK
INTO THE NEXT VOLUME OF TEAROOM MYSTERIES!

Tea and Touchdowns
BY ERIN KEELEY MARSHALL

Jan Blake held securely to the reins and nudged her horse forward with her boot as she'd been instructed.

The air was cool, even for an October Sunday afternoon, and she was glad for her gray flannel shirt and red vest. A breeze boding of coming rain draped the pasture and nearby woods in a cozy sort of gloom. Since the sun was hanging out behind thick clouds, Jan prayed the storm would hold off on this opening day of Lancaster's Fall Fest. Dry skies would also be better for sales at the merchant booths in town and at picturesque spots along the riding route.

Although Jan wasn't an experienced horsewoman, she was enjoying her mount, a gentle-natured buckskin named Triscuit. Leaves crunched beneath the hooves of a dozen horses and their riders, who were a mix of locals and tourists in town for the fall colors and the much-anticipated homecoming football game between the Forrest High Pirates and the Claremore

Raiders. As alums of Forrest High, Jan and her cousin Elaine Cook loved living back in Lancaster for this time of year.

Jan patted Triscuit's tan neck and smoothed her black mane. She was slowly feeling more comfortable in the saddle. It was good to try something new when life took a turn. She wondered what Bob was doing right then in Baltimore and smiled to herself. He'd been gone only a few weeks—he'd moved there for a job, an opportunity of a lifetime—and she knew he was adjusting to the distance as much as she was. But she was happy today, despite the deep sense of loss she'd felt since he left, and she clung to that happiness. Elaine had offered to man their Tea for Two booth on her own so Jan could take part in the first trail ride of the week. It was a generous gesture, one of many Elaine had been offering lately, Jan thought with gratitude. Elaine seemed to be very concerned for Jan's emotional state since Bob's move.

But pockets of joy were coming more and more frequently now for Jan, faster than she'd expected, and the fog she'd felt when Bob first left had begun to lift. Ultimately, she was happy for him. And she was the one who had chosen to let him go without her, after all.

She pulled gently on the rein with her right hand, and Triscuit responded by moving to the center of the trail. She looked around, glad she was still in Lancaster and not in Baltimore, glad she still owned Tea for Two with her cousin Elaine. She took a deep breath of the crisp air. Yes, she'd made the right choice.

The trail meandered through trampled meadow grasses crisping in the autumn air and into forested areas shaded by tall oaks, maples, and evergreens. The whole area included acres of three adjoining properties on the outskirts of town: the Richardson dairy farm, Dr. Tyson and Claudia McInnis's Orchard Hill, and the Donahue Stables.

An hour ago she'd driven up the winding drive of the Donahue property and seen the sprawling white house that presided over two paddocks and two large white outbuildings she learned were a barn and indoor arena. After some shuffling of horses and cinching of saddle straps, and taking instruction from the stable hands, she and the other riders were ready to go.

Jan felt as if she'd put in a full day already. First thing that morning, she and Elaine had made the easy drive in Jan's old Camry from downtown Lancaster to their booth site. They'd chosen a spot near a number of other booths in a clearing where the three properties met, accessible by a tire-worn path a hundred yards from the main road. The owners of the three properties had worked with the town's selectmen to arrange a community gathering area there for festival events.

A circular seating area had been set up with log stumps and hay bales for chairs around a large fire pit in the center. A couple of white, open-air tents had been erected nearby, with space for additional temporary seating that hadn't been delivered yet. It would be the site for the community bonfire. It would also draw people to the dairy farm's corn maze, the orchard's apple trees, the stables' trail rides, and the sales booths. Elaine was back at the booth now.

When they'd arrived there in the morning chill, Annie Richardson of Richardson's Dairy Farm was eyeballing the placement of their tables for her husband, Gavin, and his dad, Ethan, while their three kids unloaded coolers of milk and cheeses and other products they planned to sell. The What-Not and Oldies But Goodies and A Little Something stores were setting up too, and some members of the Lancaster Community Church were assembling a backdrop for puppet shows they'd put on for kids. Jan had waved to her friend and the town librarian, Priscilla Gates, who had been nestled among boxes of used books she was selling. Jan was also glad to see that Dr. Tyson and Claudia, who owned the orchard, brought along two of their employees to help set up their bulky booth, from which they'd sell all kinds of apple goods like homemade applesauce and cider. All in all, the fair had an unfussy but organized and charming feel.

She looked around again at her riding companions, most of whom were visiting with each other. Most were locals she knew, as well as a family of three—two parents and a middle school–aged daughter visiting the area. And she was delighted to share the ride with three students from Forrest High in Penzance, the school that Lancaster's teens attended.

She'd fallen behind most of the group and was now riding close to Dori Richardson, a senior at Forrest High, and another student, sandy-haired Chris Cosgrove. Chris worked at the library and had helped Elaine and her retrieve some security camera footage last year when they were investigating a crossword puzzle mystery. He was a 4.0 student and was Forrest High's quarterback as a junior last year. Until an hour ago at the stables, Jan hadn't seen him for months.

She caught their eyes and smiled at their banter about the game the next weekend. "The whole town has football fever, don't they?"

Dori grinned back from her perch on an older paint horse, and a smirk spread Chris's freckles. His lanky frame sat atop an Appaloosa. Both looked comfortable in sweatshirts, jeans, and hiking boots.

"Definitely," Dori answered. "Do you like football, Mrs. Blake?"

"I do. I've sat in the Pirates' bleachers more times than I can count. You can't beat football season around here."

They agreed, and Dori looked mischievously at Chris. "Too bad you turned traitor on us."

He made a face. "Hey now, that was my parents' fault. I got dragged into it."

Dori's ponytail bounced playfully, a little lighter brown than Jan's short cut. "I'm only teasing. Everyone misses you."

Chris must have noticed Jan's quizzical expression. "We moved to Claremore over the summer." He looked a little regretful but shrugged.

"He's QB for the Raiders now, too bad for us," Dori quipped.

"Ah." Jan made sure she looked impressed as she pushed up her glasses. "Congratulations. But I'm guessing that feels a little complicated."

"No kidding." Chris shook his head.

Jan thought it must not be easy transferring right before the last year of high school, especially to a rival like Claremore. The two schools had battled fiercely for decades, even long before she and Elaine were students at Forrest High.

"Trace and Derek are like lost puppies without you," Dori teased again, but not without a hint of support in her tone.

"Well, yeah," he chortled. "Maybe that'll make it easier to beat 'em Friday night."

Jan knew the big game was strategically scheduled to cap off the festival. Both teams were strong this year, with sights on the state tournament and more than one player from each side hopeful of college scholarships. "With your GPA, you could probably get academic *and* athletic scholarships," she suggested to Chris, hoping to cheer him.

He shrugged again. "Maybe. There are a few of us trying to get the scouts' attention." He nodded toward the third teen, who was riding ahead of them. "Trace, for one."

Jan followed his gaze toward Trace Donahue, Forrest High's star player, the quarterback who'd replaced Chris. Trace was a football field's length ahead of them, leading the group with his mother, Bridget. Trace's family owned the stables and horses. And Jan had taken instruction from Derek Jameson, the other friend Dori mentioned. He was yet another Pirates senior player and an extra hand at the stables during the busy festival week. He'd stayed back to get things ready for the next trail ride that evening. They all seemed like nice kids.

The rest of the group had rounded a bend that cut through the woods and were out of eyesight, so Jan urged her horse a little faster, and the teens kept up with her.

Suddenly Triscuit's ears pricked up. Half a breath later a horse's whinny from ahead pierced the air, followed by a scream. A flurry of birds shot out of the trees and scattered into the sky, staccato *thwaps* of their wings echoing through the air.

FROM THE
GUIDEPOSTS ARCHIVE

This story, by Constance Foster of Clearwater Beach, Florida,
originally appeared in *Guideposts*.

My friend May Haviland was a middle-aged Quaker with a
ramrod bearing and the softest brown eyes in the world.
Her Quaker ancestors had suffered persecution in early America
rather than compromise with their principles. One of those
principles was nonresistance, and it was bred into May's bones.

The Havilands were a well-to-do old family, and May was
the last of a long line of them. She lived unostentatiously in
Brooklyn but made at least one trip abroad every year. Paris
was her favorite destination and she stayed always at the same
modest pension where her habits were like clockwork. It was
well known, too, that she brought with her the family jewels
inherited from a succession of aunts and cousins.

One evening she came down to dinner intending to spend
her usual hour or two in the lobby reading newspapers. But
this night she discovered that she had forgotten her handkerchief, so after the meal she went back to her room for it.

As May opened her door, she was astounded to see a burly dark-haired man rifling her bureau drawers. Quietly May closed the door behind her and at the faint click the burglar whirled, a revolver in his hand.

"If there's one thing I dislike," she told the intruder firmly, "it's guns. Please put that thing down. I am not going to call for the police. I am going to help you because you must need whatever I have, much more than I do, if you have to steal for it."

The burglar was utterly dumbfounded when May opened the secret drawer of a small rosewood desk where her rings were hidden. She talked to him quietly, reassuringly, pressing the jewelry on him and telling him that she was sorry for him since his need was so urgent.

Suddenly the man dropped his gun to the floor, let out a low cry and fled, taking nothing.

The following day there was an unsigned note in May's mailbox. It read: "Madam, I have known only hate and fear. I can deal with them. But I was powerless before your kindness."

May told me the story later.

"Even guns," she said, "are silent in the face of love."

A NOTE FROM THE EDITORS

We hope you enjoyed Tearoom Mysteries, published by the Books and Inspirational Media Division of Guideposts, a nonprofit organization that touches millions of lives every day through products and services that inspire, encourage, help you grow in your faith, and celebrate God's love.

Thank you for making a difference with your purchase of this book, which helps fund our many outreach programs to military personnel, prisons, hospitals, nursing homes, and educational institutions.

We also create many useful and uplifting online resources. Visit Guideposts.org to read true stories of hope and inspiration, access OurPrayer network, sign up for free newsletters, download free e-books, join our Facebook community, and follow our stimulating blogs.

To learn about other Guideposts publications, including the best-selling devotional *Daily Guideposts*, go to Guideposts.org/Shop, call (800) 932-2145, or write to Guideposts, PO Box 5815, Harlan, Iowa 51593.

Sign up for the
Guideposts Fiction Newsletter

and stay up-to-date on
the fiction you love!

You'll get sneak peeks of new releases, recommendations from other Guideposts readers, and special offers just for you . . .

And it's FREE!

Just go to Guideposts.org/Newsletters
today to sign up.

Guideposts   Visit Guideposts.org/Shop
or call (800) 932-2145

Find more inspiring fiction in these best-loved Guideposts series!

Sugarcreek Amish Mysteries

Be intrigued by the suspense and joyful "aha" moments in these delightful stories. Each book in the series brings together two women of vastly different backgrounds and traditions, who realize there's much more to the "simple life" than meets the eye.

Miracles of Marble Cove

Follow four women who are drawn together to face life's challenges, support one another in faith, and experience God's amazing grace as they encounter mysterious events in the small town of Marble Cove.

Secrets of Mary's Bookshop

Delve into a cozy mystery where Mary, the owner of Mary's Mystery Bookshop, finds herself using sleuthing skills that she didn't realize she had. There are quirky characters and lots of unexpected twists and turns.

Patchwork Mysteries

Discover that life's little mysteries often have a common thread in a series where every novel contains an intriguing mystery centered around a quilt located in a beautiful New England town.

Mysteries of Silver Peak

Escape to the historic mining town of Silver Peak, Colorado, and discover how one woman's love of antiques helps her solve mysteries buried deep in the town's checkered past.

To learn more about these books, visit Guideposts.org/Shop